TITAN SONG

ALAN R HUBER

Titan Song copyright © 2009 Alan R. Huber

Copyright © 2022 Matthew Murray

Cover design: Derek Murphy

ISBN: 979-8-9857303-9-5

Quillan Publishing

431 N. Lakeshore Dr.

Lake Village, AR 71653

Printed in the United States of America

❋ Created with Vellum

Dedicated

To the memory of Alan R. Huber

CHAPTER 1

Six inches in diameter and just under a yard long, the silvery cylinder floated in the gossamer blackness of deep space, its glossy cover reflecting the myriad of unwinking stars as it tumbled lazily end-over-end. Inside, a special transmitter clicked and beeped.

Timed electronic pulses moved along small wires toward the antenna—a precisely tuned piece of coiled filament that shared a frequency with a receiver on Earth—then streaked off on a journey of more than three billion miles. The transmission arrived 4.48 minutes later at Trent Enterprises in San Diego, where the result was displayed on a continuous roll of white paper, the printer adding a bright red border to each side as it fed out.

At the alert signal, the technician on duty looked up from her novel, her brow furrowed. She watched the paper eject and saw that the transmission was from the *Princesshaul*, one of the company's cargo spacecraft. Other than the ship's iden-tification, the message was unreadable.

When the printer stopped, she reset the computer and reprinted the transmission, but the results were the same. She decided to reboot the entire system, but that, too, proved fruit-less. "Damn," she said, picking up her phone.

Mark Houston was about to leave the office for lunch when his cell sounded. He listened to the technician with a look of irritation. "I'll be right there," he said.

He exited his office and strode down the corridor. *This is crazy. I hope this isn't what it sounds like because it isn't supposed to happen. First the* Baronhaul *and now the* Princesshaul? *Something's going very wrong with those damned autobuoys.*

Near the end of the long hallway, the door to the computer room was open. The technician, standing at the printer, saw Mark's frown and moved out of his way.

Mark tore the sheet from the printer. "You rechecked this?"

"Yes, sir, three times. I even restarted the whole system to make sure the problem wasn't on our end, and it isn't."

"I don't like the look of this at all. This printout is almost the same as the one we got from *Baronhaul* last week. What the hell's going on around here?"

She shrugged. "I don't know, sir. Like before, I'll send out tracers and keep you informed."

"Good. I'm going to lunch, so get back to me in an hour when I'll be in my office."

A lot of people are in a lot of trouble, Mark realized. *A crew of forty manned the eighty-thousand ton spacecraft* Princesshaul *that, along with the* Baronhaul, *was transporting ore back to Earth from*

Saturn. It's been a week since the Baronhaul *disappeared leaving a similar garbled communication from its autobuoy. Now, a total of eighty Trent employees are missing along with a lot of raw material in two huge cargo vessels.*

Mr. Trent is not going to be happy.

"Come on in and sit down, Mark." Carl Trent indicated one of the chairs in front of the desk. "Tell me what you know about the *Princesshaul.*"

Trent's fifteenth-floor office was large and tastefully decorated with several abstract paintings hanging on dark paneled walls. Two large floor-to-ceiling windows framed the area ten feet back of the large teak desk and looked out on apartment building roofs across the street. The owner of the company, a thin man in his early seventies, stood looking out, arms folded. He turned and stretched out his hand. Mark passed him the information folder and sat down.

"There's not a whole lot to tell, sir," Mark began. "The *Princesshaul's* autobuoy shot that bunch of garble out the same way the *Baronhaul's* did, and every tracer we put out comes up with nothing. One thing I don't understand is that everybody in both of those crews has the capability to communicate individually, so we should at the least get locators, but we can't even get those. It's as if they simply vanished. The last contact, as you see, was just before the ships left Geneva Station. From what we know, the *Baronhaul* departed a couple hours before the *Princesshaul.* Everything looked normal, but now there's no sign of either one of them."

Trent took a moment to sift through the small sheaf of papers.

"Is there anything else?"

"No, sir."

"You know my grandson Eli, don't you?"

"Yes, sir, I know him." Eli Trent, early-thirties, was the head of the engineering department and one of the principal people responsible for the design of the autobuoy. Mark worked with Eli many times in the last several years and was impressed with Eli's abilities and vast technical knowledge.

"I just got through talking with Eli," Trent said. "Mark, I want you to take him with you and find those two freighters and their crews. Pick his brain. He knows every system we use, and he'll be invaluable to you. Do whatever you have to do, go wherever you need to go, and bring our people back."

"I'll sure try, sir."

"Not good enough, Mark. Take care of it."

"Yes, sir."

During the ten years Mark Houston worked for Trent Enterprises, he enjoyed the position and the constant challenge. Befitting his role as head of security, Houston was a muscular and quick-witted one hundred eighty pounds. At forty-five, he had a full head of medium brown hair above a craggy, clean-shaven face. Women saw him as handsome, charming, and having a good sense of humor. Men saw him as competitive and trustworthy, but sometimes, especially lately, a little curt.

He sat at the bar in Bud's Place—a dark, five-booth cocktail lounge a few blocks from Trent Enterprises' World Headquarters— with Eli, a slightly smaller man who was nursing his second mug of beer on a stool to Mark's left. They were going over their plans, which they agreed would have to be flexible.

Mark gently sloshed the last couple of ounces of a vodka martini in the glass between his hands, his big forearms resting on the soft black vinyl cushion that edged the polished cherrywood bar. He put the glass down on the shiny surface and twirled the toothpick between his thumb and index finger, watching the attached olive rotate in the clear liquid like a big green eyeball, its red pupil scanning the room as if searching for some understanding.

"I can't figure this out," he said. "The ships must have blown up or been hit by an asteroid or something, but they were *two hours apart*. That's sure as hell not likely. I mean, I've been thinking about it a lot, and it doesn't make sense."

"If there'd been an explosion, there'd be debris. No"—Eli shook his blond head—"there has to be some other explanation." He took a long sip of his beer. "Look, the *Princesshaul's* buoy is still sending signals, so we shouldn't have much trouble finding it. When we do, maybe we can make some sense of it all."

Mark nodded. *I sure hope so because I'll bet I could find something better to do.*

Mark's limited knowledge of the autobuoy was that it was a kind of black box for spaceships. Before the franchise system had been set up, competing shippers actually waged combat in space. The autobuoy was an attempt to thwart fighting by keeping both Earth bases and space stations informed as to the locations and functions of all ships involved in interplanetary travel. The crews' activities and physical condition were also monitored. Everything was automatic and, like the black boxes used in airlines, virtually indestructible. Eli, from behind his rimless glasses, was the brains behind the autobuoy.

"My father warned me about guys like you," Mark said, smiling. "He said you engineer types have no souls. You live so much in data that you have no inkling what it is to relate to other human beings on a personal level. You're like accountants except you deal with products that directly affect a lot of folks' lives. Accountants never see the people they do all the work for. Damn, you really are despicable."

"I hope you're kidding"—Eli shifted a little on his stool —"because otherwise, I'd have to beat the crap out of you with my slide rule."

"What? Slide rule? What the hell is that?"

Eli laughed. "Now you know why security guards are called rent-a-cops."

Mark laughed and drained his martini. "You about ready?"

"Sure." Eli drank the rest of his beer and plopped the mug down on the bar. "Let's get out of here."

CHAPTER 2

The moonlit sky was clear, but a thickening bank of September fog was stealing inland from the coast, absorbing shafts of rectangular whites and yellows into its murky body as it flowed like smoky molasses around the downtown office buildings. The balmy temperature's cool edge of humidity was driving away the last vestiges of what had been one of those perfect San Diego days. In the fall, San Diego was considered the ideal place to live weather-wise, and the Chamber of Commerce always seemed to make the most of it. Mark, however, had come to dislike nights like this one for the sting they kept bringing back.

As the corporate cop for Trent Enterprises, part of Mark's job was to catch freeloaders. A few months earlier, he had picked up a couple after weeks of searching the near planets and space lanes. After a long boring flight back, he delivered the freeloaders to the U.S. Marshall and was looking forward to seeing his wife again. That June night, too, was cloudless with ground fog and a full moon . . .

Outside the courthouse, he'd climbed into a cab. "Lakeside. Gideon Circle North," he'd told the driver, and stretched his six-foot frame across the back seat. *It's good to be home.* They headed east on Highway 94, leaving the urban population to deal with sulky corners of obscure streets.

Mark looked down at his hands. In the light of a street-lamp, he saw his palms glistening with perspiration. He rubbed them together, smiling. *Pollie, you do wicked things to me. You are one exciting woman. You're lusty and sometimes even insatiable. Now, I'm coming home. I hope you're ready.*

The taxi left the city behind, and inside the car became black. Mark closed his eyes, letting his mind pull up a scene in their Jacuzzi the night before he left . . .

While he waited for her to undress, he changed into his bathrobe and
    prepared margaritas. With a drink in each hand, he used his butt to open
    the back door and brought the glasses to the gazebo. He doffed his
    robe and slipped into the tub, luxuriating in the relaxing swirls churning
    over his naked body. He switched on the underwater lights and lay back,

letting the cares of the day fade away.

Welcome home.

He closed his eyes and hummed to himself.

A moment later he heard the screen door. He watched as Pollie came

out of the house wearing her own bathrobe—white instead of his blue—

the belt untied and loose. With each step as she approached the Jacuzzi,

she let the robe slip off her shoulders a little more. She came up the two

wooden steps at the outside edge of the tub, a playful smile dancing

across her lips, and tossed the robe aside. He watched her nearly perfect

pale body as she eased herself into the roiling liquid.

Feigning anger, she declared, "I've been waiting a long time for you

to get back."

It became a long night. They both went to bed exhausted.

Mark opened his eyes about half a block from his house and noticed a black-and-white sheriff's

shuttle parked in his driveway. That could only be Deputy Jerry Lucas, a big, rough-cut Norwegian with a ready smile whom they had befriended two years before. Jerry was now a frequent visitor. Mark was slightly annoyed. *So much for my sensuous reunion with Pollie. I'm sure the problem's minor, but he's got lousy timing*. He paid the driver, picked up his bag, and entered his house.

Jerry was in uniform standing in the entry. Two large black suitcases stood on the floor beside

him. They looked a lot like the ones Pollie used when she traveled as public relations director for her job at the insurance company.

Mark caught Jerry's eyes as he came in. "Hi, Jerry."

Jerry looked at him but did not smile. "Pollie and I are leaving, Mark."

Mark froze. He felt as if he had been punched in the solar plexus. He found it difficult to

breathe. Several seconds passed. He stared into Jerry's gray eyes, his own narrowed. "What the hell are you talking about?"

"Jerry?" Pollie called. Carrying an overnight case, she emerged from the hallway in black three-inch heels and a black-satin mini wrap with a V-neck cut to the waist where a wide gold belt cinched the wrap closed. Her smooth ivory body was a sharp contrast to the ebony satin.

"Oh—"

She hesitated, her eyes wide with surprise when she saw her husband.

Pollie, who almost never wore a bra, had maintained throughout their marriage that she would never become pregnant, that a baby would never suckle her breasts because that would ruin their form. Mark always believed that with patience he could change her attitude. Now he understood why she wanted to look so attractive. As she approached the two men, her unrestricted bosom shifted, a sight that under normal conditions would have tantalized Mark. She stopped just in front of him and reached around, handing Jerry the small piece of luggage.

Mark watched Jerry take the case and put it on the floor next to the other suitcases. As Jerry bent over, Mark noted the revolver in his holster and remembered his own pistol tucked in his belt behind him. His heart pounded in his chest as his confusion turned to cold rage.

"Aw, shit." In one motion, Mark drew his pistol and took a step back from them. Extending his arm, he aimed the nine-millimeter semi-automatic at Pollie's left breast, took off the safety, and cocked the weapon. The simple click sounded abnormally loud. "I think I'm going to kill you both."

Pollie's face drained. Standing in front of Jerry, unmoving, her breathing seemed to stop.

Jerry's eyes bulged, his brows raised. He spread his hands away from his body, palms out, saying, "Hey, man, you don't have to do this."

Mark looked over the top of the pistol into his wife's hazel eyes and saw the sheer terror she was experiencing. *She probably thinks I'm going to blow her head off. Jesus, you piss me off.* Uncounted thousands of images and memories streaked through his brain like a series of flashbulbs popping off in milliseconds. Then, his whole body seemed to calm.

"Jerry," he said, his voice low and even, "take this bitch and get the hell out of here."

Pollie hurried out the front door. Jerry picked up her luggage and followed. Neither spoke.

Mark stepped outside and watched as they got into the patrol vehicle and left. He went back inside, locked the door, and put the pistol back in his belt.

In the kitchen, he found a tumbler and a bottle of tequila. He filled the glass and drank the

contents in one swallow. The tequila caught in this throat and jumped back up into his nostrils, making him cough and causing his eyes to water.

He put the glass down and tore a paper towel from the holder attached to the underside of the cabinet. The towel's happy face design mocked him. He blew his nose into it then wiped his face. Somehow, his eyes kept watering.

Welcome home.

CHAPTER 3

After checking their baggage, Mark and Eli passed through the terminal and stepped onto the ramp area where a hundred high pressure sodium lights on high poles illuminated the last minute launch preparations. The *Catalina*, a Trent shuttle more than two hundred feet long, awaited fifty feet below the walkway.

The ship looked like a huge chrome bullet lying on its side and resting on a giant wheeled sled. Mark stopped to watch two small hovercraft, each manned by a pair of inspectors, darting in and out along the spacecraft's skin like big flies worrying a horse. One hovercraft slipped out of sight between the wheels of the sled, then reappeared a few seconds later. The other managed the fuel hose and dogged it to make sure nothing messed up the transfer. A moment later, the two vehicles stopped a few feet from each other. The inspectors, apparently satisfied, moved off. Mark left to find his seat on board.

Eli had taken an aisle seat. Mark's was next to the window

—a thick circular piece of glass about eighteen inches in diameter. They buckled their harnesses and settled in for the first leg of their flight, the two thousand miles to Alpha Station. Alpha Station was to be their staging point for the journey to Geneva via the *Traveler* and, they hoped, for the answer to many questions.

After a few minutes, they became aware that the ship had begun to move.

Mark looked out the thick glass. The *Catalina* headed down the long track and left the lighted terminal behind, picking up speed as it descended. Just after it entered the haze, the sled's motors powered up, and the ship seemed to jump ahead. The slope gradually changed from downward to upward, and the ship came out of the fog bank accelerating so rapidly that the surface lost all detail. Mark felt the g-forces compressing him into his seat and remembered the warning about tightening his abdominal muscles to keep from blacking out. He took a deep breath and pushed back.

When the forward motion reached three hundred miles per hour, the *Catalina's* own engines ignited with a tremulous roar as the ship streaked up the last mile-long section of rail, detaching from the sled and shooting into the night sky atop a magnificent four-hundred-foot plume of white fire.

The ship accelerated at a dizzying pace for several minutes as it climbed into the upper atmosphere where it finally reached escape velocity and stabilized. It seemed to Mark that the ship slowed then, though he knew that the *Catalina* was now traveling at a constant twenty-five thousand miles an hour. The pressure on their bodies relented, and he relaxed. Within an hour, they would arrive at Alpha.

As often happened when he was not busy with something else, Mark found himself musing about Pollie. *Whether I was home all the time or not wouldn't have mattered. She was good at making me think she was crazy about me. Hell, sometimes the sex was so fantastic that I believed I was the greatest lover in the world.* He snorted. *Yeah, I know there is more to it than that, but she was great at that, too. Well, some women can.*

He shook off the thoughts and closed his eyes. *Never mind.*

"Hey, Mark," Eli said, interrupting his thoughts, "the ship we're going to meet—the *Sentinel*—I think you know a couple of the crew."

"Like who?"

"The first officer is Rico Martinez."

"Hey, Rico made it? Good." Mark smiled. He and Rico, a friend for many years, had spent a lot of time at Bud's shooting pool. Occasionally they had joined forces, and, when they did, they dominated the games. They were a great team. *It'll be good to see Rico again.* "The big guy has been whipping around for a long time. I'm glad to see him get the appointment."

"Yeah, and the skipper is a lady I think you know." He paused. "Carole Banning."

Mark felt as though he had been punched in the stomach.

A long time had passed since he and Carole had gone their separate ways . . .

• • •

They first met at a Christmas party nineteen years before. Mark, then two years with Trent and a security officer, knew the instant he saw her that their relationship would be special. Indeed, the experience was an altogether uncommon one. Carole was just over five-and-a-half feet with a great figure and an infectious smile. She wore a medium-length navy blue dress with spaghetti-straps that showed a lot of skin and millions of little freckles. Pinned to the top of her bodice was a double coil of green and red ribbon. Her shoulder-length red hair complemented her deep green eyes whose irises were sprinkled with tiny gold speckles that created a mesmerizing effect, which, once experienced close up, Mark would never forget. She was studying flight engineering at the time, one of a number of people who were working to get into Trent Enterprises' new planetary operations.

Introduced by Carl Trent, she greeted Mark with a handshake that was firm and warm. At her touch, his body became awash with a feeling he could only think of as an invisible warm shower. Nearly a hundred other employees were in the convention hall, including a band that was tuning up, but at that moment, they seemed to melt into a silent background. He had never met a woman who affected him so quickly.

"A pleasure to meet you," he replied.

Carl pushed them lightly together with his hands on their backs and said, "I'll leave you folks to get acquainted. Have a nice Christmas."

They thanked him, returned the holiday wish, and watched him walk away.

When their eyes met again, the shower feeling restarted in

him. They said nothing for a moment while he searched her face. "Did you feel that?" Mark asked.

He knew it was forward of him, and he expected her to ask him what he meant or to have some sort of evasion. He was surprised and pleased that her eyes sparkled as she smiled and said, "Yes, I did."

"Let's sit down. Can I get you something to drink?"

"Yes, tequila, please." She settled herself on a loveseat along the wall just behind them.

"Okay, I'll be right back."

He returned and sat next to her, setting a small tray on the coffee table in front of them. He had her drink and a tequila of his own to which he'd added a shaker of salt, a slice of lemon, and a paring knife.

"May I show you something?"

"Sure," Carole said.

"If you like tequila, you'll enjoy this. A Mexican friend told me the original 'shooter' was made not with lime, but with lemon, and they did it like this—"

He picked up the knife and cut the quarter-inch thick slice of lemon into three wedges. He shook some salt on one of the triangles and licked it off, took a third of the tequila into his mouth, and re-salted the piece of lemon. Before he swallowed the tequila, he sloshed it around inside his mouth for a few seconds. As soon as the liquor went down his throat, he bit the pulp from the wedge and chewed, then swallowed it to follow the tequila. Finally he took a deep breath.

"They don't do the ritual with lemon anymore because most bars don't keep the rind with pulp but just the rind itself to use as a garnish with a few drinks," Mark explained. "Bars do have chunks of lime, though, so people started using limes. Limes are okay, but the effect of tequila as a liquor is better with lemon. Tequila was really meant to be sipped—and it is strong that way—but as a shooter like I just did, it's possible to get feeling pretty good with just a jigger. You do it more than three times and you're going to be surprised."

"And tipsy, I guess, hmm?"

"You'll feel it, I guarantee. That's because moving the tequila around in your mouth allows it to start to vaporize, so when you breathe in, the vapors are absorbed more quickly. I suppose you could call it a cheap drunk because even though it costs a lot less to get inebriated this way, the effect is greater. Want to try it?"

"Absolutely."

The band was good. They danced that night to a few fast tunes, then some slower songs. Toward the end of the evening, they tried the shooter once more. When the music stopped at the last dance, he put his hand under her chin and lifted her face. Just before she closed her eyes, he noticed those little bits of gold. She did not pull away. As he kissed her, he felt her arms around his waist and her body pressing into his.

After the party, they walked the two blocks from the hall to Mark's apartment, a little drunk and glowing with happiness. Neither spoke as they came in. He closed the door and started to switch on the light, but she put her hand on his wrist.

"The nightlight's enough," she whispered.

When he reached around her to lock the door, she put her hands, one on each side of his face, and pulled his head down to her. Her lips were warm and delicious. While they embraced, he slipped his hands onto her shoulders and under the straps of her dress. She shrugged the dress off and let it fall to the floor. The contrast of her black bra and panties with her pale skin seemed perfect; the whole image of her aroused him.

During the intense, sensuous night, they napped once for a few minutes before finally falling asleep with approaching dawn . . .

Yeah, I know her, he thought. *It's been a while, though. With our different schedules, our paths never crossed again, and then Pollie came along.* Mark had to admit that his memory of Carole had faded as he tried to imagine what she would look like now. *We all change over time.*

Mark watched the forward monitor as a huge silver disk came into view. At a mile across, Delta Station floated in space like some gigantic wheel a little more than halfway between Earth and Saturn, rotating at a speed that gave the outer ring simulated Earth gravity for the hundreds of people living and working there. The center was a large hub that provided parking, loading, and unloading facilities. A dozen spokes housed elevators for transit from the hub to the great ring—a combination of residences, recreation areas, workstations, and laboratories.

The *Catalina* decelerated as it approached the station and came to a stop within a few hundred feet of the hub's main doors. Six small shuttlecraft jetted out to nudge the big ship into the proper position the way tugboats guide an ocean liner to a pier. The place they picked to tether the *Catalina* was next to a much smaller, sleeker vessel with bright blue letters on its side: *Sentinel* - Trent Enterprises.

The two men disembarked with the crowd and took the workstations' elevator. Just inside the exit door they found the directory. Eli looked up the whereabouts of the *Sentinel* crew and called them. He explained the situation, then turned to Mark.

"That's Rico on the other end," he said. "They'd like us to come to their quarters in an hour. Sound good to you?"

"Fine. That'll give us time to get cleaned up."

CHAPTER 4

Rico Martinez opened the door. At just six feet, he was the same height as Mark but outweighed him by a good forty pounds. His dark brown eyes crinkled. Wearing a broad smile, he reached out a large hand. "Hello, Mark. God, it's great to see you again! How are you?"

The place was a like a ship's stateroom with only one small window in the wall to the left that looked like any porthole Mark had ever seen. Stepping from the small entry into the main room, he noticed the cabin's walls were covered with a light brown paneling that offered little personality to the otherwise stark accommodation. A large oval table with connected stools dominated the first half of the room. A man and a woman sat on two of the padded chairs located in the other half.

"You look good, Rico. It's been about a year, hasn't it? Don't you ever get tired of floating around out here?"

"Hey, man, you work hard, you get rewards." He indicated his collar with three gold stars.

"I heard. Congratulations. When are you heading back?"

"The way it looks now, probably another month or so. Warm up the sticks."

Mark grinned, envisioning this hulk of a man bending over green felt, poised for a dead-eye shot on the eight ball. As partners, they were almost unbeatable. "Bud said to say hi to you. You left me in the lurch, I hope you realize. I've lost a lot of money since you took off."

"Mark, Mark," Rico said with a mock frown, "don't worry. We'll get it back." He turned and stretched out his hand to the other man. "You must be Eli Trent. It's a pleasure to meet you." He indicated the other two in the room. "Let me introduce you: Dr. Karen Bradley and Engineer Jim Conry, meet Mr. Eli Trent and my old friend, Mark Houston."

Doctor Bradley was a heavy woman of about thirty with long brown hair, dancing blue eyes and an infectious smile. She was of necessity a general practitioner, able to handle almost any kind of medical problem. Her hand was strong with a firm shake. I'd feel comfortable in her care, Mark thought.

The *Sentinel's* engineer was a smaller, younger version of Rico but with a weak handshake. Mark was surprised, but dismissed it. Maybe it was just all that working with numbers and machinery—or maybe Conroy was just tired.

"Captain Banning will be out in a moment," Rico said. "The others are next door. Can I get you fellas something?"

Mark requested iced tea, and they moved to the table.

"Say, what you been up to lately?" Rico asked.

"Oh, I've been busy enough," Mark said. "When I'm not rounding up stowaways, I'm training the new guards and doing some private stuff—not that I need the money, but it keeps things from getting too boring."

"How'd they get you in on this?"

"I'm going to arrest the bad guys, Rico, and bring them to justice." He smiled. "I'm looking for anything that would explain the disappearances. Even out here, it's pretty hard to make big spacecraft like the *Baronhaul* and *Princesshaul* just vanish. One thing we'd like to do is get hold of one of the autologs. All the info they transmitted was junk."

"Mark's got it about right," Eli said. "Apparently the autologs malfunctioned. If I can take a close look at one, I may be able to figure out what went wrong. But we're supposed to check out the problem with Geneva first."

"You guys get to take us out to Geneva," Mark added, "so we can find out what's going on out there."

"I'd like you both to meet the rest of the crew," Rico said. "The captain will join us shortly for the briefing."

The door at the back of the room opened. Mark watched an auburn-haired woman enter carrying a small red notebook computer. She wore a light blue uniform dress with four stars on the collar.

Rico nodded to her. "Good evening, Captain."

Mark stared. Carole's hair was shorter than he remembered —just above the collar—but otherwise, she appeared as if the intervening years had never taken place. Her face was a soft oval of smooth, lightly-freckled skin dominated by those wondrous emerald eyes with tiny bits of gold that you had to be very close to see. Her delicate nose had a subtle bump midway down, then gave way to a small point before refashioning into a sensuous mouth with a slight overbite and naturally red lips that she never needed to decorate. At five-and-a-half feet, she carried a hundred twenty pounds with a quiet and unpretentious assurance. Mark felt himself flush and wondered if the others saw it.

Carole glanced around the table and their eyes met. At first he felt ashamed that he had not been able to keep a perfect picture of those beautiful green eyes in his memory all this time, but he forgave himself immediately. *Ten years is a long time.*

She approached Rico, who introduced her to Eli. After they shook hands, Rico turned to Mark. "Captain Banning, Mark Houston."

"We know each other." She grasped Mark's hand. "How have you been, Mark?"

Her hand seemed too warm to him. Its warmth spread through him to his abdomen. The subtle vapor of vanilla reached his nostrils, a long-forgotten aroma that rekindled memories of their intimacy, and now the warmth grabbed his groin. Mark had presented her with a gift of that perfume after their first dinner together, and that night their lovemaking reached a level of passion beyond anything he had previously known. Aware of how it affected him, thereafter she wore it in tantalizing ways, applying it to the most sensuous parts of her body, even under the most sedate circumstances. *I love to tease you,* she said, *because I enjoy the benefits.* He felt complimented that she still favored the fragrance, and wondered if she was wearing it for his enjoyment now.

"It's good to see you again," he said, choosing the words to sound casual. "You've come up in the world, Captain. I hope we'll have a moment to talk."

"Thank you. I'm sure we will." She addressed the gathering. "Please, everyone, sit down."

She began with an overview of what had taken place in the last few days, including the attempts by the *Sentinel* to find anything that would indicate what had happened to the *Baronhaul* and the *Princesshaul.*

"The *Traveler,* our sister ship, is probably on Geneva, but we haven't been able to verify that. Our first task is to get to Geneva Station and find out what's going on there with the communications. You can understand the concern—it's been almost two weeks since anyone's been in contact with them."

A call from the communications center interrupted Carole's presentation. They relayed an urgent message for Mark from Carl Trent. Carole suggested he take the call in the next room, so he excused himself, closing the door.

From the time markers at the top, he knew the call was a videotape. Given the distance from Earth, a live conversation would take almost half an hour each way. He wondered what might be so important. Carl Trent's face materialized on the monitor.

"Mark, I'm sorry to give you bad news." Trent paused. "Your wife has been in an accident, and she's in bad shape. She was a passenger in a helocar that crashed heading into downtown in the fog. Apparently, the blades of the roto clipped a building, and the chopper caught fire on impact. A couple of people tried to help them. The driver was trapped inside and burned beyond recognition. Mrs. Houston was rescued, but she was badly burned. I've already arranged for your return on the *Catalina*, which I delayed for this purpose. They'll let us know as soon as you arrive here, and I'll send a shuttle for you. She's at Kensington Hospital under Dr. Gregory Draper's care. I suggest you go directly to the hospital and contact me afterward."

Mark stood, silent, staring at the screen. "To replay message, touch (R). To end, touch (Z)."

He recalled Pollie's look of indifference as she left with Jerry Lucas, and the memory made him consider whether or not he should tell Trent to forget the return flight. Embarrassed by the feeling, he sent Trent a short message saying he would be returning forthwith and rejoined the others.

"My wife has been in an accident," he told them. "She's in Kensington Hospital. It's pretty bad, and I have to leave right away. Eli, your father has booked me for immediate return on the *Catalina*."

"I'm sorry to hear, my friend," Eli said. "I hope everything will be okay. Anything I can do?"

"No, but thanks. I'd better get going. They're waiting for me."

Carole walked with him as he turned to leave the compartment. At the door, she stepped in front of him. He stopped and looked down at her. Her eyes were soft and gentle, and he saw comfort and genuine concern. She reached up and put her finger to his lips, then drew his head down to her and kissed him on the cheek.

CHAPTER 5

Six days in suspended animation passed as an instant for him. The arrangements had been taken care of: the Trent car met the *Catalina* and carried him directly to the hospital where he entered the lobby and walked to the information desk.

A pretty young brunette, whose blouse bore the ubiquitous happy face and a large white badge with the name Bonnie, looked up as he approached. With a manufactured smile she asked, "What can I do for you?"

"I'm Mark Houston. My wife, Pollie, was in a traffic accident about a week ago, and I need to see her. Doctor Draper is in charge."

Bonnie's smile evaporated as a more serious expression transformed her face. "I'll call Doctor Draper. Please have a seat."

Gregory Draper had been their family physician for the last three years. Mark knew his wife was in capable hands, but when they talked on his way in, Draper's tone was ominous.

"She was burned over ninety percent of her body, Mark. She's in intensive care. Her condition is critical. I don't know how much longer she'll hold on."

The elevator doors opened. A tall man in his mid-fifties stepped into the lounge area. His thick hair, aging in a salt-and-pepper way from the deep black it had been when his life was less complicated, was brushed in a long curve around and behind his ears. His eyebrows, having never compromised their color, splashed across his forehead without a pause as if they refused to be though of as two separate lines. Combined with eyes like two chunks of coal and a pencil-thin moustache just below his straight Saxon nose, Gregory Draper's gaze had an innate power of great authority.

Spotting Mark, he joined him, his hand extended. "I'm sorry to see you under these circumstances. I know you've had a long trip—would you like to sit and have a cup of coffee?"

"No, thanks, Doctor. I'd like you to fill me in on what you know."

"Pollie is on the third floor. I warn you; it won't be pleasant."

"I understand. Let's go."

In the elevator, Draper explained that Pollie was in flotation because of the severe burns to

almost her entire body. "Most people don't realize how frightening serious burns are, and when other injuries are present, to look is difficult. I'm not trying to be morbid, Mark. I just want to prepare you for what you'll see."

29

"I appreciate that, Doctor."

Draper talked of the machinery connected to her and the way her skin was mottled: black and high pink and white. Mark listened with mixed feelings.

When they arrived at the ICU, Draper led him to her room and stopped outside the door. He scanned the monitor. "I'll wait here. Go on in."

Mark entered what looked like a small theater, albeit one filled with that super-clean, vaguely ozonic odor of technological wizardry. The lighting was subdued, coming from fixtures behind valances along the upper edges of the sedate green walls. In the center of the fifteen-by-fifteen room was a table upon which lay the nude form of his wife, face up. She was completely encased in a series of transparent liquid-filled tubes. The support equipment, hooked up to her from the ceiling, looked like some monstrous multicolored spider web emitting soft buzzes and clicks. The almost inaudible rhythmic swishing of the flotation tubes moved in cadence with her measured breathing. He took a slow full breath and stepped closer.

Despite Draper's attempts to prepare him, what he saw dismayed him and brought a wave of sympathy for her. Except for a blood-reddened bandage wrapped around the top of her head and one more on her stomach, the only skin not charred or blistered was her chest. Those haughty breasts, firm and stark, were floating undamaged in the clear fluid among all that terrible destruction. Her face, stripped of lashes and eyebrows by the flames, was bloated and bright red, her closed eyes sunken by the swelling of the surrounding tissue.

The rest of her body was torn and bruised with flaps of damaged skin floating inside the liquid, making him think of the ripped flesh of a fish he had once seen floating dead in a river. He felt his skin crawling under his shirt along with a strong sense of shame and pity.

He leaned over her, resting his right hand lightly on the plastic above her left shoulder, taking care not to touch her skin. "Pollie," he whispered. No reaction. He tried again, a little louder, but saw nothing change. Shifting position so he would be in her line of sight, he said her name again. Her eyes were open, but they didn't seem able to focus, and her gaze appeared dull.

He managed a small smile, not wanting to show her the truth that threatened to overwhelm him, the truth that he did not long for her to make it.

He returned with the doctor to his office where Draper invited him to take a seat on an old cloth couch, then went to a wet bar on the other side of the room. "What can I get you?" he asked, opening the ornate doors. When he got no response, Draper waited.

Mark was staring at the floor in front of his feet. After a few moments, he looked up. "Oh! I'm sorry. Tequila, if you have some. Tell me, who was driving the helocar?"

Three vertical lines above his nose split Draper's thick eyebrows into a deep frown. "He was burned beyond recognition. The police said the car belonged to one of their own, a deputy sheriff named Jerry Lucas."

A half-smile that he didn't try to hide crossed Mark's lips. "Oh, really? That was her boyfriend."

"I see." The doctor's expression was noncommittal. "That explains a lot. I mean, I was concerned that you didn't show much emotion about the accident. Did this happen recently?"

"A couple of months ago. For me, it was unexpected. I guess the handwriting was there, but I just never looked at the wall." He thanked Draper for the tequila and sipped some. "Tell me, Doctor. what are the chances of her getting through this?"

"She's stable, Mark. These kinds of burns do a great deal of damage, even more than you can see. And with that much of her body involved, it could take a long time—maybe years—before she comes out of it."

"What about for now?"

"She'll probably reman in a coma for several weeks at least. Her body is broken and needs to repair itself as much as it can. All I can say is there's nothing you or anyone else can do but keep her clean and comfortable. She's getting all the medicine and care humanly possible."

I have to go back to work. There's too much shit here for me to handle, and I'm not going to deal with it.

"Doctor Draper, I'm in the middle of an important project that I have to get back to. I want you to let me know the minute there are any significant changes. Call Trent Enterprises. They'll get the message to me."

"All right, Mark. I'll keep you informed."

CHAPTER 6

As he left the hospital, Mark felt the chill in the night air. He drove out of the lot, navigating the streets automatically, trying to understand the mixed thoughts that swam unbidden in and out of his mind.

Pollie was in big trouble. That she would survive seemed unlikely. *What am I supposed to do now? I just can't help feeling — what is it — satisfaction it was Jerry driving the helocar.*

That son-of-a-bitch.

What was strange was he didn't feel what he thought he should feel: worried, lonely, torn. Instead, what he was experiencing felt suspiciously like relief.

Jesus, what the hell does that mean?

He knew the answer to that, too. The six years were a sham, for both of them. *We already crossed that bridge.*

And there was Carole, coming back into his life—or was she? *I don't know anything about her now. A little wishful thinking going on here?* No, the look she gave him when he left—there was no doubt in his mind about that. And he knew something else: he wanted to see her again.

So who's the real son-of-a-bitch?

More than an hour later, he found himself standing on the sidewalk outside Bud's Place. Directly ahead of him, a few yards from the front of the bar, was a sewer grate. He stared at the wisps of steam that floated up, dissipating in the quiet, windless night. He watched the mists of tiny substance break away from the confines of the thicker curls of smoky white and then drift upward, disintegrating into the cool dark atmosphere, free of any definition or concept of form.

He shook his head.

That night, Mark talked and Bud listened. A lot of words were bandied about, and for the next few hours, they ground them up. Bud became not just the bar's owner, but a caring confidant who helped him get very drunk. At two fifteen in the morning, he called a trusted friend who, with Bud's help, poured Mark into his car.

"Make sure Mark gets safely into bed," Bud told the friend.

Mark didn't remember much with the notable exception that he got up sometime during night. With a tight grip on the toilet, quite certain he was about to fall off the earth, he vomited and begged God to help him.

Later, he wept with a great deep quaking of his chest and shoulders amid tears that burned his cheeks. The next morning, his heart, his head, and his stomach muscles hurt.

To convince Carl Trent he was fit to go on took some doing, but two days later, he was aboard the *Catalina* once more.

. . .

Doctor Draper's efforts were successful in that Mrs. Houston held on for more than a week while her body consumed enormous amounts of painkillers. On the tenth day after Mark reported back to work, Draper was paged to the ICU. Unable to prevent death, he and an ICU nurse watched Pollie in her final moments. After she exhaled her last shuddering breath, the nurse checked her vital signs. As Mark lifted each eyelid to check pupil reaction, they noted that the dark brown irises did not move. He checked each of them twice.

"Wait a second," he said to the nurse. He stepped back to the chart, flipped to the second page, and read her statistics. "Hair: black. Eyes: hazel. Sure," he said. He went to look again. Pollie's eye color was indeed hazel. He looked at the nurse, who met his gaze.

"Yes, Doctor," she said, "I did see that."

Doctor Draper returned to his office. "Trent Enterprises? I need to get a message to Mr. Mark Houston. Can you help me?"

"Who is calling, please?" the female voice said.

Draper identified himself, and the operator explained that Mr. Houston was not on-site. He told her he knew that, that the message was urgent, and that Mr. Houston was to call Doctor

Draper immediately. The operator promised she would pass the message along and that Mr. Houston would get it. Draper took her name and made a note of the time. Then he called Mark's home and left a message there as well.

CHAPTER 7

Mark stepped through the *Catalina's* airlock and into the *Sentinel's* to find Eli waiting. Mr. Trent had ordered the *Catalina* to meet the *Sentinel* directly. His explanation had been brief and to the point: "Time is of the essence."

"Welcome back, Mark," Eli said. "You look a little scruffy. What did you do, sleep all the way?"

Mark felt the stubble on his chin. "I guess I'd better get cleaned up. What's the latest on the search?"

"We don't have much. We followed what should have been the tracks of both missing freighters, but we haven't been able to find anything—not the autobuoys or anything else. The only thing left is to go to Geneva. We were just waiting for you. We still haven't been able to raise them. C'mon, I'll show you to your cabin."

After shaving and showering, Mark changed to a denim shirt

and slacks and made his way to the bridge, which was crowded with equipment except for the area directly in front of the captain's position where Carole Banning sat in a black bodysuit. Her chair was flanked by that of the communications officer on her left and Rico Martinez on her right. Five feet in front of her was a large square viewscreen that extended from the ceiling to within two feet of the floor. In its upper left corner was a reference picture of Geneva Station, while the main part of the screen, dead center, showed the planet Saturn the size of a golf ball.

Rico saw Mark standing at the hatch and pointed him out to Carole who waved him forward.

"Hello, Mark." Her voice was even. "Glad to have you back."

"Thanks. Eli said you haven't had any luck with Geneva yet. How long before we get there?"

She pointed at the image in front of her. "We should be there in two hours. The station will swing into view just as we arrive."

"The last thing the boss said to me before I left was he hoped Geneva Station hadn't disappeared, too."

Carole smiled. "Oh, it's there, all right."

"Have you heard anything from the *Traveler*?"

"No, but it's possible they're inside and working on the problem."

"If I were the skipper of the *Traveler*, and the problem was nothing more than communications, I would have sent a message with my ship's radio."

"Yeah," Carole said, "I suppose it didn't occur to him. By

the way, I have something to show you." She rose from her seat. "Rico, we'll be in my cabin."

The captain's quarters on the *Sentinel* were smaller than Mark imagined—not much larger than an average living room. Every wall was covered with what appeared to be natural dark mahogany paneling. A mahogany conference table and attached chairs occupied the front half. A large desk that featured a computer terminal dominated a raised area, a step up, not quite in the center of the room. The desk backed up to the far wall where several plaques proclaimed Carole's educational and professional qualifications. In the exact center of the wall was a flight safety award given by Trent. The award was a silver-plated square, edged in gold, and bonded to a backing of polished teak. The award cited Carole Banning's one million miles of piloting without an incident and bore the four stars of her rank.

The door slid closed. Carole stepped past him and went to a cabinet on the wall beside the desk. Her mood seemed almost formal. "Tequila?"

"Yes, thank you. I'm surprised you remembered."

She poured two tumblers. "Oh, I sample some now and then myself," she said, handing him a glass.

She sat on the edge of the desk, half-on and half-off, her left toe just touching the deep carpet. Mark walked to her. They touched glasses, each taking a large sip. He indicated the plaque on the wall behind her. "I'm impressed, but not all that surprised. I knew you were a good pilot then."

"I've missed you." With her head bowed and in a voice so

low he almost didn't hear, she added, "And over the last few years, I've called you some really bad names."

"I'm not sure I deserve that. Carole, I don't know if—"

"If what?" She looked up at him, one eyebrow lifted. "Are you going to tell me now that you feel differently because she's in the hospital?"

"No, I'm not going to be a hypocrite about it."

"Good. I think I know what your marriage was like, Mark, because I, too, had one that wasn't so good. I'm familiar with the mental cruelty, the evasions, and the inability to make the decision that should be made. It's living a total damned lie, and you gave me the strength to stop doing that. Our lives should have been together, and the reason it didn't happen is that we didn't want it bad enough." She sipped her drink. "What I want to know is"—she probed the center of his chest with her index finger—"what's in here."

He took a deep, slow breath. "You already know that. It's never changed, Carole. But what the hell am I supposed to do? You want me to divorce Pollie right now, while she's in a coma?"

"It isn't what I want, Mark. It's what you want that matters."

He was quiet for a long minute. Finally he said, "I'm having some very unnerving thoughts." He wanted to fill his arms with her. He wanted to press her close to him, to touch her hair, to hold her and not let her go. He wanted to ravage her.

Instead, he took her hand and closed it between his palms, while looking into her eyes. They were beginning to shine with an increase in moisture that threatened to spill over. He kissed each of them with a tenderness like a feather. It belied his feelings, his mind gnashing with anger at this untenable situation, at his lifetime of stupidity and wrong headedness. He did not deserve this seething, this torment.

"Mark . . ."

It was only one word, but it told him what he needed to know. It soothed him, and it healed him. The anguish faded. He would not let this second chance die.

"Please don't tempt me," he said. "I don't think I have the strength to resist you."

"My heart says there's no reason for you to resist. I love you, Mark. I always have." She pulled her hand from his and threw her arms around his neck, her breathing deep and full.

Her body was again pressed to his, after so long away for so many years. Mark felt the warmth, the pleasure, and the urgency, and his arms encompassed her as he had so many times before. She made it sound so simple, so easy, so good.

They were alone together, and she lifted her face. Mark bent his head to see her, her face that was angelic to him. Her eyes were closed, and two small rivulets of tears traced their way from the corners down her soft cheeks. His heart seemed to swell in his chest, and he drank in her face with his eyes. Her lips parted, and he touched them with his, tentative at first, just a brushing contact, and Carole moaned from her chest. He felt it more than heard it. Her arms pulled his face to hers, and their lips met, tasting each other fully this time, with a release of the hunger they had been feeling, a hunger that had been forestalled all this time. Her lips were glorious and

40

moving and inviting and delightful and wanton, and he succumbed to it all.

They held each other, nearly unmoving, for what seemed a timeless ecstasy. They breathed together, their cheeks against each other, and each said the other's name, once—in slow motion, a star going nova, a galactic event of enormous magnitude.

Later, they began to unravel almost as if they had been of a single mind. They watched each other's glowing face as they parted, with a reluctance that was almost palpable. The process was long. Neither said a word, as if they each knew nothing needed to be said at that moment.

CHAPTER 8

When Draper arrived in his office the next morning, several packages sat on hisdesk. One held the information he needed. He reached over and slid the big yellow envelope from the stack and sat down.

The envelope had been sent by courier from the office of Dr. Reginald Hawthorne, the pathologist who had performed the autopsy on Pollie Houston. Hawthorne was a thorough and efficient man of many years' experience. Draper had known him for quite a few of those years when they had worked side by side on more than one occasion. He had total confidence in Hawthorne's expertise.

Draper picked up his letter opener and slit the envelope flap, dropping the contents onto his desk. A large manila folder slid out, inside of which were several sheets of paper and a small video cassette. This last would show the entire procedure. He swiveled in his chair and introduced the cassette into his player, then switched it on. The holograph displayed a few feet in front of him, about a quarter actual size. He adjusted the settings so the image was half normal size.

Nothing was unusual for the first thirty minutes, so Draper fast-forwarded through, the impressions flashing in front of him. When the brain was being dissected and analyzed, something caught his trained eye. Doctor Hawthorne mentioned a small, brown, tumor-like body within the folds of the rear portion of the left cortex. Because Hawthorne went through the analysis in such a matter-of-fact way, Draper almost missed it. The video showed the little lump along with the other portions of the brain, but Draper had to stop the cassette to study it. Hawthorne mentioned the lump only in passing, as if it had no significance. *That's strange,* Draper thought. *Any kind of anomaly should be detailed.* He decided to call Hawthorne.

He picked up the phone and punched in the number. Within seconds, the other man's desk and upper body appeared on the screen. He looked tanned and fit.

"Reggie," Draper said, "how are you doing?"

"Pretty good, Greg. Been busy today, but it won't keep me from enjoying the weekend. What's going on?"

"I was looking at the Pollie Houston autopsy, and I noticed something. When you were examining the brain, you went through it pretty fast. I saw a small brown mass that you removed from the left rear section of the cranium. You hardly mentioned it."

"So?"

"Weren't you a little curious? I've never seen anything like that, and I just wondered why—"

"Whoa, Greg. Are you trying to say I don't know what I'm doing?"

Draper realized his tone sounded accusatory. He shifted in his chair. "Sorry. I didn't mean to insinuate anything, but you dismissed it without even a comment. I have to sign off on all these forms, and I just need to be clear on it, that's all. Can you tell me about it?"

"Sure." Hawthorne became cool, authoritative. "In the last twenty years or so, I've seen several similar to it in human brains, cadaver and otherwise. The exact area in the brain where that lump was located has no significant effect on human behavior, as far as is known. It's one of those areas that's never used, that's all. In clinical tests, electrodes inserted into a number of spots in the cortex and other portions of the brain record no activity. There's a theory that this represents evolution waiting for us—that someday, those areas might be used in things like extrasensory perception or an ability like mental telepathy or telekinesis."

"You mean mind over matter?"

"Right. It's a fascinating possibility. Fortunately for us, small internal damage or tumors like that one, in those particular spots, never seem to become a problem. In the distant future, I suppose, when much larger portions of our brains are developed, head injury of any kind will probably be of much greater concern than it is now. Of course, all that's just speculation, but I like the theory. Hey, I'd love to be around when those things come about."

"Maybe, if your field were psychiatry. A lot of crazy people will be running around when you start reading minds."

"If you think women have power now, imagine the power they'll have then."

"Answer one question for me, will you?"

"Sure. Hey, why don't you and Debbie come on over and watch the game with us? Bring a six pack. I already have the pretzels and stuff."

"Yeah, sounds like a plan. Let me see what she's got going on, and I'll let you know. But back to the subject. That part of the brain—where you got that tumor—doesn't that have something to do with vision?"

"No, but they're next door neighbors."

CHAPTER 9

Even from eighty thousand miles away, just the idea of that great steel satellite, that tiny black dot above Saturn's colorful surface, was awesome to Mark. He found himself impatient, wanting to see how people lived and worked inside a huge metal ball. He remembered reading somewhere that clouds actually appeared inside on occasion, and once in a while, it actually rained. An amused smile danced across his face at the mental image of a bunch of workers skipping around in puddles doing Gene Kelly impressions. *Well, you've got to have entertainment, right?*

Carole reported back to Trent that they intended to set down on Geneva Station. The *Sentinel*
slowed to a thousand miles per hour as they approached. Rico reported the distance, closing from less than five hundred miles. Mark and Eli sat on the bridge watching the forward viewscreen, fascinated. The tremendous fifty-mile-across globe

seemed implausible, hanging in space, twenty thousand miles above Saturn's equator. The rings surrounding the planet angled from lower left to upper right and looked like a beautiful phonograph record, incredibly thin and fragile to the eye. Mark knew, however, that any craft passing through them could be stripped of its outer skin, sand-blasted by dust particles, or torn to pieces colliding with boulders hundreds of feet or more across.

"Two hundred fifty miles," Rico said. The satellite now took up almost the entire screen, reflecting the great planet's gaseous upper atmosphere on its polished surface. The ship was nearing the only structures on the outside of Geneva, the communication buildings, that showed no lights, no movement, no signs of life.

"All stop," Carole commanded. "Magnify, maximum."

Drifting to a position directly over the primary communications building, Carole brought the *Sentinel* to a stop forty miles above the surface. Geneva's proximity radar antennae, designed to detect any object larger than a pea, were unmoving. The sensor probe display showed nothing but the walls and rooms and the structure of the compound itself, no images of human beings.

"I don't like this at all," Carole said. "We'd bet—"

The bridge shuddered and heaved as though the ship had been struck by a giant ocean wave. A high-pitched screech began, and just below the viewscreen, an area about the size of a quarter became incandescent. The screen went black.

"We've got an electrical problem," Martinez said.

"Go to it," the captain told him.

A shower of sparks spewed into the room as if someone on the other side was cutting the bulkhead with a welding torch. The spot started to move down toward the floor, leaving a blackened slice in the wall with air rushing out into space through the opening.

"What the hell—" Banning gripped her chair's arms and leaned forward, her face reflecting her puzzlement.

Martinez ran to a compartment in the side wall and jerked open the door. He grabbed a canvas bag from inside and spilled its contents on the floor. Tearing the corner of a large fat envelope, he began squeezing the filler near the wall's open slice. The thick clay compound was sucked from the envelope like a snake, but the smoldering edges of the bulkhead kept it from adhering.

As the cut reached the floor, it erupted with a small explosion. A shimmering white beam extended from the floor completely through the bridge into the ceiling, screaming through the air just past Martinez's face.

Mark's heart pounded. He realized if the beam struck any major wiring, the ship could be uncontrollable. He also knew that in a few minutes, the bridge would be void of air.

Carole hesitated no longer. She opened the ship's address system. "This is the Captain. We have an emergency—all hands abandon ship immediately." She repeated the message, activated the evacuation alarm, and jumped from her seat, yelling, "Forget it, Rico! Clear the bridge, and take Eli with you. Let's go!"

As the others strode out the exit, Mark reached for Carole's hand. The air supply was already getting thin, and he was sure they only had a few seconds left.

"Wait!" Rushing back to the captain's chair, she pushed a set of four buttons on the control panel then raced back to him, shoving him through the doorway ahead of her. When she was one step outside, she spun around and closed the hatch.

"Why did you go back?" Mark asked.

"I released the autobuoy. Come on, the modules are below."

They ran down the passage with Carole in the lead. Making their way down one more level, they reached Bay Number One. The mysterious destructive beam was already ripping a line in the walls as they climbed into the extravehicular module, a tight-fitting two-seater shuttlecraft.

Carole powered up the module and opened the *Sentinel's* outer doors. She went through a radio check with the other members of the crew, telling each to rendezvous on the station's surface. Then she worked the controls so that the little unit lifted off the deck and streaked out of the ship's port side.

Twenty miles away, as the unit continued to accelerate, she enabled the rear camera. Mark watched, his heart racing. Things were moving too fast, and his mind hadn't yet caught up with what was happening.

The monitor magnified the picture, zooming in until the *Sentinel* filled the screen. A series of small explosions shook the stricken ship. The sides of the craft bent inward, and the entire vessel seemed to collapse in on itself, as if someone had attached a giant suction device to the nose of the ship. In the next instant, it erupted with a blinding white flash. The camera field went to one-to-one, and they watched the explosion expand into a mile wide sphere. In one more second, the explosion dissipated into the blackness of space.

The *Sentinel* was no more.

CHAPTER 10

For the first moments following the destruction of the *Sentinel,* Mark felt total loss. When his heart began to slow and his breathing became more regular, his mind started to toy with the idea that they were going to die. Intellectually, he had tried to deal with the possibility that something like this might happen ever since he first began working with Trent Enterprises.

He had been in situations that were dangerous, but never in one where he truly felt that he might not survive. The reality was much more fearful than anything he had conjured in his head. The situation seemed to make him hyper-sensitive to his body and created a completely encompassing force around him, almost like heat. His mind was gripped with a firm realization that after death there is no awareness. To shake the thoughts off took a substantial effort.

Carole brought the module to a stop. She attempted to contact the other crew members with no replies.

"Mark, did you see where that beam came from?"

"No, I couldn't tell."

"I saw it cut off just before the ship blew up. It was coming from Geneva."

He stared at her. "Then somebody's taken over the station."

"We have to find out."

"Wait a minute—you're not planning to land there, are you?" He didn't like the idea of confronting someone who had firepower like they had just witnessed.

"You have a better idea?"

"Maybe," he said. "What about going home?"

"This thing has the capability to suspend us, if that's what you mean," she said. "We could head back, and hope someone finds us. We'll probably be a little older."

"I can't think of a single objection to sleeping with you for a few years. Not one."

Carole ignored the remark. "You want to leave the others?"

He felt angry at himself for making the comment. The fact that the comment truly reflected his feelings was somehow not important. He had always had little respect for men who were controlled by their genitals, and he had just done it himself. He said nothing.

"Well, then, sweetheart, I guess you'll have to take a raincheck on the slumber party." Her face, now serious, turned toward the front. "Let's go find them."

As they approached Geneva, Mark noticed that the station rotated on an axis perpendicular to Saturn's surface. *The place is a marvel.* When he had been told to go with Eli, he decided he'd better learn as much as he could about the ships, the cargo route, and Geneva. The holographs he saw made him feel tremendous respect for the people who put the gigantic project together.

The inside of the immense satellite was filled with grid-work that was used to get from place to place. All the crew quarters, family areas, power plant, vehicle storage, administration and other facilities had been built on the inside, but communications functions were added to the outer surface. Most cargo transfers were carried on inside the huge tube that ran through the center of the sphere where gravity was at a minimum. The tube could be flooded with air, so loading and unloading could be done without the need for spacesuits. The winged remotely-controlled rockets carrying ore came in through the doors closest to the planet's surface, termed the "south." Once loaded, the big cargo haulers exited the "north."

Carole brought the module in a wide arc around to the south, darting in an irregular zigzag to evade any possible tracking. She kept the shuttle at a gradually declining slope until they were ten feet above the surface. She focused on the instruments, watching for the override panel that would be located just a few yards from the doors.

"Carole, I think you'd better stop."

"What's the matter?" She glanced at him.

He pointed to the left side of the viewport, outside her line of sight. "Look."

She leaned forward and looked out. The horizon showed a great concave gap. She steered toward it. As they drifted closer, they realized that this hole in Geneva's shell was created by the south polar doors, already in the open position. Moving at a crawl to the edge, she let the craft nudge over the opening, then hover.

They watched the landing lights inside pulse invitingly, blinking in sequence in several lines from the quarter-mile wide doorway deep into the dark interior, stopping at the airlock door three miles away. Other guide lights circling the sides gave Mark the impression of a gigantic spider web.

"Come into my parlor," Mark intoned. "I think I know how that fly felt."

"We don't have much choice. One thing is certain: those door didn't open by themselves. Regardless, we can't sit out here."

"Whenever you're ready, honey."

CHAPTER 11

"Mr. Trent, Ed Masterson here, in Communications."

Masterson's voice had a foreboding edge that Carl Trent could feel through the phone. Thirty years earlier, he had received a call from his father with the same flavor to it. He knew when he heard his father's voice he was about to hear something unfortunate had happened. His father needed only to identify himself, and Carl sense the mood as if it had been a mist of hot water. He thought it must be about someone they knew, that something had happened to a family friend or relative.

"Carl," his father had said, "I have some bad news for you."

"What's happened, Dad?"

"Son, your mother is dead."

The enormous implication of what he heard did not register in his brain. He remembered now that his response had been *which one*. He had misunderstood, or, more accurately, his brain had changed the words he heard to *your brother is dead*. He had three brothers, and it later became clear to him that his mind simply refused to believe that his mother had died in favor of the lesser catastrophe that one of his siblings had. The quirk had been burned into his consciousness, and it came back now as he heard Ed Masterson's voice. He steeled himself for such a bulletin.

"The *Sentinel* was apparently destroyed a few hours ago," Masterson said. "We think everyone got out safely, but we haven't heard anything since. There is indication that the ship began to break up, but exactly how or why is not clear. We're sending the *Monitor* and *Vikinghaul* to the area, and a couple of other ships in the vicinity will join the effort to find the crew. They must need fuel, which means they probably went to Geneva. We still haven't been able to contact the station, so that's all we know."

Trent wanted to question Masterson, to ask him about Eli and about anything else he might know, but he knew that Masterson would have said anything else there was to tell. He thought about how frightening it must be drifting or lost in the vastness of space, millions of miles from any humans. He himself had been on one space flight that had serious problems, and the passengers were so panic-stricken they froze.

The experience reminded him of the wildebeest in the Serengeti being brought down by the lioness. Even though the wildebeest has many times the strength of the big cat, once the lioness has it by the throat and begins to strangle it, the wildebeest stops struggling and goes into a sort of shock, as though it has resigned itself to its fate. It loses its will to fight, to survive, and simply accepts its end—as did the passengers on the ship Trent was on. He remembered thinking they should be screaming and milling around, but they instinctively knew that being in a crippled spacecraft somewhere between the earth and the moon was equivalent to the wildebeest's position. To get up and run served no useful purpose since there was nowhere to go. Nothing could be done about what had happened. Their fate was in someone else's hands, and their rescue, occasioned by the passage of another ship nearby, was a stroke of total luck.

When Ed had gone, Trent crossed the expanse of dark green carpeting and stood alone, gazing out the window at the night sky.

CHAPTER 12

Carole turned the nose of the module into the huge hole. Proceeding slowly, she inverted the craft a few yards above the inside surface of the entry so they could see the black steel directly through the small front window of their vehicle. The enormous size of the place made it seem like they were a tiny bug crawling down the barrel of a cannon.

Carole switched on the exterior lights, including the seep headlight. She adjusted the headlight so it illuminated a bright swath in a fan shape twenty feet in front of them. "I'm looking for one of the work hatches. They're located about every hundred yards or so. Let me know—wait, there's one, just ahead."

She rotated the vehicle right side up and edged it to within a few feet of the ten-by-ten foot door, then hovered. After a moment's consultation with the computer, she poised her finger over the pad. "Ready?"

"Go ahead," Mark said. She touched the final key and the hatch slid to one side, revealing a dark space beyond. She made another set of entries and the walls inside the little station illuminated with a dim red glow.

Carole parked the module inside, closed the lock, and began to pressurize the compartment. They traded looks of relief as the hiss of air stopped, indicating normal atmosphere.

"In that satchel just behind your seat are a couple of hammer guns, Mark. Get them and hand me one."

Surprised, Mark stared at her. Hammer guns, which were modifications of the old, more cumbersome laser pistol, were outlawed except for specific uses. They were the first small hand-held weapons that employed the principle of molecular disintegration. Any living organism struck by the beam was progressively destroyed, regardless of where it was hit. If the target was an inanimate object, it simply put a hole in it, the depth depending on the range set on the weapon when fired. This unforgiving and devastating piece of armament was deadly, and, according to what he had heard, nothing could stand up against a hammer gun. Supposedly the gun had gotten its nickname from a quip of the inventor, something to the effect that having a weapon like this was like using a hammer on a cockroach. Whatever, the name stuck.

Carole met his gaze and seemed to read his mind. "Mark, captains of monitors are authorized. A list of possibilities was foreseen."

"Like what—alien T-Rexes?"

She laughed. "Maybe, I don't know. We all had the option, and I thought the guns might be useful sometime."

Mark reached back and retrieved the two guns from the pouch. Before giving one to Carole, he looked at them for a moment. He had never seen one up close.

"They're semi-automatic," she told him, her voice matter-of-fact. She pointed out the small window on the gun's top that indicated how many shots were left, adding that a fully-charged pistol had a capacity for thirty firings. "You have to pull the trigger for each burst. Don't forget to set the range. I put mine at maximum, about a hundred yards. The beam is yellow colloidal, so you can see it even in a vacuum. If you miss the first time, you usually don't have much trouble correcting it." She indicated the satchel again. "Oh, pick up a couple of reloads, too. Those are the slides that fit into the slots in the bottom of the grips."

Mark toyed with the clip, thinking how much it resembled that of an old Colt .45, then slipped the clip into his pocket. He felt some apprehension as he fingered the awesome weapon. He sighed and stuck the pistol into his belt.

Armed, they exited the module. Carole worked the keypad that opened the inside airlock door, and they stepped into Workstation Number 168. The hatch opposite them was open to the interior of the station. They moved to the ten-foot square opening and paused to listen. The entire sphere, almost two thousand cubic miles, was dark and still.

"Wait a minute," Mark whispered. "The entry light is on, and the airlock works, so there has to be a source of power—but I don't hear anything."

Carole stuck her pistol into her waistband. "Go back to the

EM. You'll find a couple of flashlights in the back section behind my seat."

"I'll be right back." He took the few steps to the parked vehicle and opened the far side. Retrieving the two flashlights, he switched one on and started back.

Halfway, Mark stopped. He moved the light in quick searching circles. The glossy white walls of the workstation bounced the beam of the flashlight around the space revealing the hundreds of rivet heads, cable runs, control boxes—every inch of the interior—in sharp detail. The shiny bare metal of the empty hatchway stood in stark contrast to the blackness beyond.

He was alone.

CHAPTER 13

I'm Dr. Gregory Draper, here to see Dr. Cameron Lloyd," he announced to the young receptionist. "He's expecting me."

"One moment, please." She spoke into her earpiece, then told him Doctor Lloyd would be right down.

Cameron Lloyd was in his early sixties and head of Kensington Laboratories' research department, which occupied a large building next to Kensington Hospital. His credentials, as Draper already knew, were unquestionable and his integrity beyond reproach. A tall slender man with slightly graying red hair, he wore wire-rimmed glasses and sported a thick red moustache.

As the elevator lifted them to the twelfth floor, Lloyd said, "This specimen that you called about that came out of the lady's head—we've had a helluva time trying to figure out what it is. I hope you can shed some light on the thing. As you'll see, it has some unusual properties. For one thing, we can't seem to cut it—Ah, here we are."

They went through a door labeled "Experimental: Obtain Special Entry Permission" below which were Lloyd's name and phone extension. Inside, the room was lined with cabinets and glass display cases of various types and sizes. They stopped in front of one small case. "There's your little mystery. I'll get us some gloves and show you what I mean."

When they had donned surgical gloves and masks, the lanky redhead stuck a bony hand into the case and removed the lone item in the petri dish to a white ceramic table in the middle of the room. He slid a drawer open, paused, and selected a standard scalpel.

"Watch this." He took the rubber-like material from the dish between his thumb and forefinger and placed it on the table in front of them. He set the scalpel just above it and brought it down until the sharp edge touched the upper surface. As he began to apply pressure, the blade made a small impression, but when he started a sawing motion, the entire mass seemed to slide to one side to evade the scalpel's edge. No cut was visible.

Lloyd turned to Draper. "Would you like to try?"

Puzzled, Draper took the scalpel and bent over the white ceramic table. He took the specimen in his hand and uttered a surprised grunt. "This thing must weigh over a hundred grams."

"Yes, we noticed that." He smiled. "Actually, it comes up just short of two hundred."

Draper attempted unsuccessfully to slice the specimen. The scalpel would not make an incision. He tried once more, then again. On the last attempt, the knife slit through the thin surface of his glove, taking the very tip off and almost cleaving his own fingertip. The specimen remained intact.

"Wait a minute—that's impossible." Draper tried again with the same result. "Have you tried the laser?"

"Oh, sure. The same thing happens—I mean, it just avoids being cut. It's as though it detects what's coming and takes evasive action, but it's not alive." He picked up the piece of flesh and returned it to the petri dish, covering it. "We also tried X-raying it and got nothing. Then we tried soundscan, MRI, and finally stuck it under the thetascope—and still, zippo. Doctor, we don't know what the hell that thing is."

"I don't know, either, and I don't understand." Draper stroked his chin, deep in thought. "All I know is Doctor Hawthorne removed this specimen from Mrs. Houston's head. The area in which he found it was next to the part of the brain that controls vision. He said he's seen things like this before but never thought much of it. As far as he knew, the tumor never affected the patients physically. Possibly the tumor's having that little connecting thread means there's some correlation between this thing and the eye color change."

"Do you think this tumor had something to do with Mrs. Houston's death?"

"I don't know. Everything is speculative right now. I don't doubt Hawthorne's conclusions, but I think I'll talk to him again. Something's fishy."

Draper bounced the tumor in his palm. "Doctor Lloyd, I want you to freeze this thing so we can take another look at it later. Would you do that?"

"Why freeze it?"

"Well, for one thing, we might be able to cut it."

CHAPTER 14

T his is impossible. Carole was here just a moment ago. She must have fallen in—but why didn't she scream? Maybe she hit her head or something . . .

Mark pushed the flashlight beam into the darkness. A few yards ahead, a ramp fell away from the bottom of the door frame, then turned to the left. A five-foot-high chain link fence ran along both sides. A thick cable strung through the top row of links appeared to support the fence and ramp.

She couldn't have just disappeared. I could go back to the module and leave. One way or another, I could figure out how to navigate the craft and even activate the hibernation system and get back home.

Mark knew that was not an option. Carole was missing, and he had to find her.

He held onto the door frame and again stabbed the light into the blackness. The ramp led to a walkway that stretched into the darkness. The four-foot-wide, steel ribbon walkway was hung with hundreds of beams and cables that joined a gigantic web of ladders, other pathways and small buildings as far as he could see. Two canvas-covered strands on either side of the walkway just above waist level served as handrails.

At the end of the ramp, Mark extended his foot and stepped out. His first tentative steps were wary, but when the structure did not quiver, he gained confidence. He stuck his weapon into his waistband and began to walk normally, careful to keep one hand on the rail. His ears strained for the slightest sound. A distant humming, perhaps from a generator of some kind, was so low-pitched he had to strain to hear it. Its steadiness was almost soothing.

A hundred yards inside, he stopped, switched off the flashlight, and returned it to his back pocket. He didn't like the idea of advertising his presence with the light. Knowing night vision would take about ten minutes to come to him, he grasped the side rail with both hands and waited.

A dull thumping came to his ears, raising the hairs on the back of his neck. With every sense in his body heightened, he slowly turned at the waist, holding his breath. The thumps seemed to slow as he turned. He decided the unseen danger, whatever it was, could detect his movement and seemed cautious when he was. He heard the slight rustle of his clothing as he shifted back toward the other direction, and the thumping slowed even more. A chill wave crossed his shoulders and ended in his chest. With every molecule of his body alerted, he was ready to weather whatever attack would come.

He let out his breath in a slow, quiet way, and the thumping became faster, then fade—

Damn, that's my own heartbeat! There's nobody here! In the darkness, an embarrassed smile crossed his face. He was so relieved he wanted to laugh. *God, this place is so quiet, it's like a tomb.* His smile faded at his bad choice of words.

He waited a few more moments to satisfy himself that he was indeed alone before bringing out the flashlight and switching it back—

He lurched backward as his leg jerked out from under him.

Off balance and in a near panic, he reached for the rail. He missed with his right hand, but his left arm found it, and he crooked his elbow around it. Something that felt like a thick rope coiled around his ankle was wrapping itself around his right leg and pulling him almost horizontally, threatening to tear the limb from his body. His heart throbbed wildly. His left arm screamed for relief. Unable to hold on, he released the railing. He flew through the air and slammed down on his back. The flashlight flew down the walkway, its beam whipping in crazy patterns until it bounded against the chain link and came to rest shining back at him.

He looked down. A moving cable was winding itself like a serpent further up his leg as it pulled him. The other end was over the handrail a few yards back from where he had stood. The cable yanked him sliding on his back into the netting and pulled him upside down toward the top of the chain link. He braced his free leg on the bottom of the rail to stop from being dragged up and over it, his muscles protesting as they were tested to their limits. He grimaced at the excruciating pain, sure his leg was about to be torn off.

Wrenching the pistol from his waistband, he swung it toward the snare and squeezed the trigger. A yellow flash—

and the beam flew past the top of the fencing. He corrected his aim, and a second shot severed the bottom two wraps of the snake-like cable. The parted end stopped moving as the other portion slipped back into the darkness. Released, Mark fell to the walk on his back.

He removed the smoking coils from his leg. Rubbing his sore back and flexing his arms, he strode the few yards down the walkway where he recovered his flashlight and shined it on the fistful of remnants. What he beheld in his hand was some sort of curious cable or metallic rope slightly thicker than his thumb and perhaps four feet long. The particle beam had cut cleanly. Small bits of electronics and wires were visible, and a trace of some sort of grease. He threw the cable off the walkway. It whirled gently, struck something with a light clink, and continued on its twenty-five mile drop.

He heard something else—a swishing sound—and spun around again. His searching light beam quickly found the source of the noise. A long cylindrical object twenty-five feet in diameter was suspended among the cables of the gridwork. The cylinder was over a hundred feet long and angled away from him toward the right. Perched on the cylinder's near end was something the size of a car that looked like a huge blob of mercury. The blob shimmered in a beautiful, fragile, almost hypnotic way as it reflected the light in pulsating waves. Emanating from various points on the cylinder was a series of long, stringy arms snaking through the air in all directions. Mark watched, fascinated, as the object seemed to swim within itself, its movements almost like breathing. Mark felt a sense of well-being and became rapt, staring at the smooth surface.

This machine is the most beautiful I have ever seen.

He stood unmoving, his eyes fixed on the center of the glob, unaware of what was happening. The stringy arms swung in larger and larger arcs, whipping the air, its sounds almost musical. One arm missed his head by inches and wrapped itself around a support cable just beside him. A second arched above him and behind his head, the tip dropping between his shirt and back. In an instant, the arm coiled around his shoulder and, slithering like a hungry snake, wrapped itself around his neck. The arm tightened—and still Mark felt only an uncaring throb, an inner beat like that of a bass drum. A feeling of goodwill wafted over him and descended upon him like a pall. He felt a solace, and wanted to feel the soft texture of the surface in front of him.

The loss of his ability to breathe and the strictures on his neck were reducing the amount of oxygen getting to his brain. Still he was unconcerned because the music was his favorite, one of Wagner's old classical themes he'd loved from his youth. He was caught up in the all-encompassing cymbal crashes and bass drum rolls . . . *This is absolutely wonderful . . .* He closed his eyes to better feel and enjoy the music.

Inside his eyelids, he saw a tiny white dot. The dot seemed to swell, then recede, then swell again. With each cycle, the dot became larger, continuing to grow until, after a few more pulses, it became an enormous starburst with rays of white cosmic matter streaming from the central point. Without warning, the music stopped. The starburst turned red, and a high-pitched wail pierced his ears. The wail screamed into his mind, and his body began to spasm.

Mark's eyes opened and sent the picture they beheld, despite the slowing of most of his other body functions. From somewhere deep inside his brain, a tiny message jumped the last synapse and screamed along an electrical pathway that if the muscles of his arms and hands didn't do something, his body would be useless in short order.

His right hand crawled along the waistband of his slacks like a wounded spider. He located the butt of the hammer gun and slipped it out into the open air. The first squeeze of the trigger seemed to Mark to require two minutes to manage. He could feel every whorl and ridge on his fingertips and every fiber of every muscle involved in the motion. The yellow flash was as bright as if the gun had gone off inside his head. He did not understand that the shot stopped him from being strangled until he saw the rope-like tentacle dangling from his chest.

Sucking a great *WHOOSH* of air into his oxygen-deprived body, he fired a second shot that hit the blob in the middle. The blob projected a child's scream into Mark's head. The small wound the beam made expanded, smoldering and cooking at its edges. His chest heaved and his legs trembled with weakness as he watched the entire mass reduce to a boiling slough in a few seconds, chinks of it dropping away into the blackness. The reality struck him: with a single pull of the trigger, he had doomed the thing—whatever it was—to annihilation. There was no wounding or incapacitating with this weapon. *One shot, and you're gone.*

71

The silvery-brown cylinder seemed to be a telescope of some kind—but that didn't make sense. The nearest part of the station's shell was almost a mile away. Then he noticed that the cylinder was pointed in the direction from which the *Sentinel* had come.

Mark raised the hammer gun. With careful aim, he placed two shots into the laser cannon. Whatever mechanisms they struck sparked and smoked.

Certain that he had disabled the cylinder, he continue down the walkway.

CHAPTER 15

Reggie, you said you've seen those little tumors in lots of brain cavities over the years, and you've never found them to be malignant. You said, too, that you felt they had no effect on the people who were carrying them around." Gregory Draper was sitting in Hawthorne's office.

"That's right. What's bothering you about that?"

"I'm not sure. Before Pollie Houston, when was the last time you saw one of these things?"

"Oh, hell, I guess it was about six or eight months ago. An elderly couple in Las Vegas was at a blackjack table—doing pretty good, I understand. Anyway, he fell off the stool in cardiac arrest. I happened to be in the same room, so I rushed to the man's side and tried CPR for quite a while, but it was obviously too late.

"The man's wife asked for an autopsy, and, because I was

available, the Las Vegas coroner asked me to perform it. I confirmed the cause of death, and there was no further question."

"And you found the same sort of thing in his head?" Draper leaned forward. "Was it exactly the same?"

"Sure, but, as I said, nothing about it was remarkable. I've seen a lot of them."

Draper was getting anxious. "Wait a minute. Just how many of those tumors have you seen, altogether?"

"I'd say about a dozen or so, over the past twenty years. My God, Greg, I've probably performed five or six hundred autopsies in the length of time. So what?"

"Hang on, hang on. Do you have records of all of those autopsies where you found this type of tumor?"

"Yes, you know we have to keep them forever. I even had to get a copy of the one I did in Vegas, so I could add it to the vault here."

"Okay, one last question. Has anyone ever done lab tests on the specimens before?"

"I don't know. I never asked for one. I didn't ask for tests in Mrs. Houston's case, either." His thick brows pulled together in a thoughtful frown. "Wait a minute. Yes, my assistant did. She's a young intern with a lot of gung-ho. She insisted, even when I told her it was unimportant, that I'd seen them before. She asked if it would be okay, and I said it would be. I think she was curious because of the weight and the feel of it or something. She sent a sample out to Kensington. All right, Greg. Can I know what the hell's going on here? Why all the interrogation?"

Draper responded with another question. "Will you give me permission to look at all the records of your autopsies in which you found those lumps?"

"Yeah, on one condition: you tell me what this is all about."

"I promise I will as soon as I figure it out myself. Look, Reggie, I really don't know anything for certain. All I have is this feeling that somehow all the people who have had this condition are tied together in some way. I haven't any idea how, but one thing I have to find out is whether or not anyone was present when those people actually died."

"Well, I know the old lady was with her husband when he died in the casino."

"Reggie, was any mention made of his eyes turning brown?"

"Oh, for Chrissake, Greg, are you still on that kick? Anyway, as I remember, his eyes were brown."

"You said you never asked for lab tests on these tumors. How could you be so sure they were harmless if you never ran tests?"

"I think I did run a test or two in the beginning, but they never showed anything. Hell, I remember taking one out of a woman's head a couple years ago, during the cleanup of an injury she sustained in a traffic accident. She was still alive and survived the whole thing, but I think that was one time I just trashed the thing. I had gotten to the point by then that I recognized the phenomenon, and that it was simply a harmless anomaly. How many 'final' questions to you have, anyway?"

"I'm sorry," Draper said, extending his hand. "Listen, I

really appreciate all the information, and I'll get back with you if I can ever put all this stuff together."

"Please do. I'd be extremely interested."

CHAPTER 16

With each step further inside the station, Mark's senses seemed to become more acute. The air seemed to get warmer, accompanied by the ever-present generator hum coming from somewhere in the bowels of Geneva Station. He realized that using the flashlight was dangerous, so he kept it off except to flash it whenever he was unsure of his direction. What unnerved him most was that all the cables supporting the walkways bore close resemblance to the one that grabbed him before. To imagine them coming alive and reaching for him was not difficult.

At the intersection of two walkways, he encountered a large booth attached to a long rectangular shaft that dropped below him for miles. With his pistol pointed at the door, he pushed the entry button. The space inside was a lobby with a double interior door he knew would be the elevator. On the right side was a directory panel. He was pleasantly surprised when he touched the panel to see it light up. He directed the panel to show a plan of the station.

The plan indicated where he was and asked where he wanted to go. Mark considered, then entered "Engineering." The plan showed Engineering's location and which elevators, walkways, and shuttles he needed to take to get there. In addition, a small note flashed:

Clearance Required — See Station Director. All Habitability Functions Automatic.

"Right," Mark said aloud. "Your functions are working perfectly. Where the hell are the lights? And have you noticed it's getting a little warm in here? Looks like somebody screwed up your programming."

His next inquiry was for a kitchen. The map showed Galley Number Eight just a hundred yards away. Gratified, he left the booth and made his way to the galley. The medium-sized building's floor was unlocked. Once inside, he made sure the building was unoccupied, then found the main kitchen. In one of the big cabinets, he found some bread and a can of something that passed for filling. It was tricky, but he managed to make a couple of sandwiches with the stuff, which tasted like minced ham. *How is it that the light switches don't work, but the refrigerators and other appliances seem to be functioning normally?* He was even tempted to cook something, but thought the smell might bring unwelcome guests.

After he had eaten, Mark felt stronger and more assured. He exited the building, his ears straining for the tiniest sound and his hand ready to turn his weapon on anything that seemed threatening. The muffled steps of this soft-soled shoes, a sound that would have gone unnoticed under ordinary circumstances, seemed too loud to make it possible to find his way unheard.

The Engineering Building was a large three-story facility suspended halfway between the middle of the station and the inner skin, requiring him to take three elevators and two shuttle cars inside long tubes that would have induced claustrophobia in most people. He wondered if the testing of the prospective occupants of this place included that little question.

Returning to the elevator, he hesitated, knowing that once inside, he could be at the mercy of whoever or whatever was in control. Having no other option, he stepped inside.

"Okay, here goes." He pushed the button for his destination.

The elevator ran almost without a sound. Fifteen minutes later, after several transfers, Mark arrived just outside the big building. When the elevator doors opened, he had his weapon in his hand. He waited a few seconds, then put the pistol back in his waistband. Flicking the flashlight for just an instant, he imprinted what he saw in his mind's eye, then walked to the front door.

He fumbled with the keypad at the entrance. After a few tries, it whispered open. Inside, he found the other panel and closed the door. The next few compartments were dark. From what he had been able to see from the outside, he guessed the place was a couple hundred feet square. He figured he was somewhere near the center, and found himself in front of yet another door. He conquered the lock and the door opened onto a dimly lit great hall with about fifty rows of tab—

Nude human beings lay on their backs upon the tables. Staring at the rows nearest him, he saw that they were alive; their eyes were open, and they were breathing. Each body was held down by the same sort of cable he had encountered, wrapped five or six times around. The cables thickened as they left each person and trailed toward the base of a single, quivering silver mass in the middle of the room where they all melded. The mass, the size of a small house, looked like a larger version of the creature he met earlier.

A single, whip-like tentacle six inches thick arched out from the top of the mass and hovered, dancing and bobbing like a twenty-foot long rattlesnake, over one of the bodies on a table at the far end of the room. Pistol in hand, Mark crept along the wall, passing five rows of tables. The cables wrapped around the people lying on the tables were not tight to the body, yet the people did not move or struggle. All were staring straight up as if drugged.

No one else was in the room. The only sound was a low hum coming from the strange entity in the center of the roo—

WHI-I-I-I-I-NE!

Startled, he looked in the direction of the upraised tentacle from where the high-pitched shriek came. The end of the tentacle had lowered, so he couldn't see what was happening. After a few seconds, the mewling stopped. The tentacle raised up and moved to the next table.

When the whining began again, he quickly skirted along

the side wall of the room until he was a few rows away from the machine's next subject. Now his view was unimpeded. This time, the victim was a woman. A foot away from her, the end of the tentacle was divided into three slender cables. One cable was pushing on her nipple, and a small trickle of blood flowed from her breast onto the tabletop.

The second cable had a small cup at its end. The cup, poised over her left eye, dropped onto her face. Mark heard a small pop and was horrified to see the cup moving up with the woman's eyeball inside.

The second cable pulled an inch away, and the third arm of this hellish triad slowly thrust itself into the woman's eye socket, through the small mass of tendons and connections and blood. The whining continued for a few seconds as Mark watched, frozen in disbelief. The third cable withdrew, and the second replaced her eye as the first pulled out of the woman's breast.

Both cables that entered the woman's body were tipped with what appeared to be long, thin, flexible tubes. Their withdrawal from her flesh brought a small cloud of smoke, and the bleeding stopped. Throughout the entire procedure, the woman had not flinched.

Mark's body trembled from nausea and disgust. He squeezed his eyes shut as his arms and hands shook. His stomach was roiling, and he thought he was about to throw up. This scene was just too bizarre, too incredible. He could not believe what he had witnessed and stood, transfixed, unable to grasp what had happened.

Impossible. You can't take someone's eye out like that and just put it back.

The noise started again. The monstrous machinery had moved to the next table. Once more its peculiar bouncing motion began above the body strapped there, another woman who, with a mind-wrenching jolt, Mark recognized—

Carole.

CHAPTER 17

Mrs. Mattox? Mrs. Benjamin Mattox?" Draper extended his hand holding his identification and stepped back to allow the elderly woman to see him in the porch light as she stood beside her partially-open front door.

"Yes," she answered through the screen door.

"Mrs. Mattox, I'm Dr. Gregory Draper of St. James Hospital in San Diego. I called you this afternoon."

"Oh, yes, Doctor." She reached for the lock on the screen door. "Please, come in."

She wore a prim white blouse with a small ruffle at the closed neck and a long, pink skirt printed with big, multicolored flowers and with one huge pocket in the middle. From the records, Draper knew she must be in her late seventies, but Mrs. Mattox gave the vital and intelligent impression of a much younger woman. He recognized the inside of her home as one of the old modular types built about thirty years before.

Warmly furnished in the colonial style, its florals and colors seemed to complement its owner.

After she offered coffee and he declined, Draper sat on the couch. Mrs. Mattox slid into an old cherrywood rocking chair that she set it in motion with a slight push of her foot. She smiled and asked, "How can I help you, Doctor Draper?"

He reviewed what he knew of the Las Vegas incident and said he was investigating one or two aspects from a medical standpoint, though he did not mention the lump that had been found in Mr. Mattox's head. She listened, nodding remembrance of the night her husband died.

"Mrs. Mattox, I need to ask you a couple of questions," Draper said. "They may sound strange to you, but it may be helpful if you can recall exactly what went on. What did happen on that trip? Mr. Mattox died on the first day you arrived, didn't he?"

She shifted in her chair, then continued to rock. "Ben and I were always very close," she began. "We went everywhere together, you know—even to the store. On our trip—to Vegas, I mean—the only time we were apart was when we were actually at the casinos. He likes to play blackjack and roulette, and I spend my time at the slot machines. The only time other time, besides that, you know, we were at that place right on the California-Nevada line, and—I forgot to tell you that we went with some friends—and at that one place on the state line, we did get separated because Ben and Ed went to play while May and I, we played the slots. But we had a deal, you know, where if we got separated we'd meet at the hotel in Vegas.

"Well, that day, the second day, May and I—May's Ed's wife—we were having such a good time and doing really well, we wanted to stay longer. Ben and Ed wanted to go on, so we said we'd meet at the hotel like we'd planned, and later we did. I guess that's all . . ."

"How long was it between the time they left for Las Vegas and when you saw them again?"

"Oh, I don't know, Doctor. I suppose three hours or so. It's about one hundred miles to the hotel from that casino on the state line—now, you know, maybe it was more like four hours or a little more. You really don't have much track or time in casinos because they don't have clocks, you know. Anyway, as far as I was concerned, nothing was unusual."

"Okay, Mrs. Mattox. Now, you were with your husband when he had the heart attack, weren't you?"

She stopped rocking. "I told him years ago to stop that accursed pipe. He smoked that thing as much as he could. Even though I wouldn't let him smoke in the house, he'd go outside and puff away on that stupid thing." She paused.

"Yes, ma'am."

"His favorite music," she continued, "was that rock 'n' roll from—God, I don't know—a hundred years ago or more? Let me tell you, Doctor, one thing that kept him young was listening to the music of the Creedence Clear River Rifles and the Beach Boys. He'd play some of that, and then he'd laugh and say, 'You're my surfer girl' and I'd laugh, too. He sure was a loving man, Ben was . . ."

"Creedence Clearwater Revival."

"What?"

"The other group—you mean Creedence Clearwater Revival."

"Oh, yes." She smiled. "Never could get that name straight. Where'd it come from, anyway? You like that rock-'n'roll, too?"

"Oh, sure," Draper said. "I inherited some original records from my father. Some of them are almost a hundred years old."

"Yes. Ben had some old tapes, too. We'd listen to them once in a while." Without warning, her eyes filled with tears that poured down her face in two solid streams, along her cheeks and chin, soaking into the ruffle at her neck. She made no attempt to stop them.

"I cradled his head in my lap," Mrs. Mattox said. "He looked up at me and tried to say something. A lot of people were around, you know, so I couldn't hear him. I said, 'What, honey?' I bent real close to him, and he just looked at me full in the face, then said real soft but kind of strong, too, 'I love you, Birdie.'"

She stopped, her eyes welling up again. "My name is Robin, but he always called me Birdie. He was a wonderful man, Ben was. We were married forty-eight years, Doctor. It wasn't perfect, but through it all, we stuck together . . . Are you married?"

"Yes, I am. It's only been a couple of years. I have another question for you, Mrs. Mattox. Even though I've gone over the autopsy report, and I know the answer, I have a good reason for asking, and it's really important to me. Your husband's eyes were brown, weren't they?"

She assured him they were, but for just an instant, for a fleeting second, Draper saw something in her face, some sort of puzzlement—and then it was gone. It was enough.

"I'm sorry to have taken you through this memory again, but I have one more question. I don't want you to think I'll think you're crazy if you say what I think you're going to say. Mrs. Mattox, your husband died right there in the casino, on the floor. Did you see anything peculiar in those last few seconds? Did you notice anything about his eyes?"

Again she met his gaze, and he could almost read what must have been going on in her mind. She didn't respond at once. When she did, she began with a preamble.

"Doctor Draper, my husband was a scientist. In all the years we were together, he urged me to be precise about things, as much as I could. He helped build Moonglow Station, that resort out there halfway between here and Mars. He was always a stickler for detail, and I guess I got it by osmosis, you know." Her eyes narrowed.

"I guess I thought I imagined it until maybe right now, but his eyes got almost black they were so dark. I mean, just after he spoke to me, his eyes widened—and just like that, they got real dark. I'm not a doctor or anything, and I'd never seen anyone die before, so I suppose I just thought that was a natural thing. But now you're going to tell me it wasn't?"

"That's right, Mrs. Mattox. It wasn't normal, but I can't tell you I know what it was. I think I know what it wasn't, and it wasn't a disease of some kind. Right now, all I know is that a number of people have been found to have had the same thing, and I'm trying to find out what it's all about." He thanked her for her hospitality and information. "If I do figure this all out, I promise I'll let you know."

Driving away, one thing kept nagging at him. Reggie Hawthorne, who kept running into this strange phenomenon through all these years, at first didn't remember ever having done any tests on it. No doctor worth his salt would ever let such a discovery go without looking into it. Yet he considered it relatively unimportant, even when he had a sample in hand.

Draper, something is rotten in Denmark.

CHAPTER 18

E d, what the hell have you been doing? It's been
almost thirty-six hours, and you don't have
anything to report?" Carl Trent paced angrily in
front of his huge desk, his chief of communications standing a
few feet away. "We have every damned ship in the area whipping around out there, and nobody has seen hide nor hair of
my grandson—or anyone else, for that matter. All we know is
the *Sentinel* is gone, and there's no word from

Geneva Station. Is that it?"

"Yes, sir. We know they got out," Masterson said, momentarily cowed by Trent's ruminating. He knew he had little to
say to placate Trent, but he tried. "Look, Mr. Trent, it's possible
they decided to sleep it out and just head the escape modules
this way. They have that capability."

"Why would they do that, with the station within shouting
distance?"

This exchange was not going well. "I don't know, sir, but

then we don't know why Geneva isn't answering." Masterson shrugged. "We're doing everything we can, sir. I'm sorry the news isn't better."

Trent walked over to the big windows, staring out and up into the heavens. He breathed a slow sigh and turned around. His voice lowered, almost to a whisper. "I know you guys are trying everything. I just keep wondering if this will turn out to be disappearance number three, and I don't know if I could handle that, Ed. My wife is frantic, and I'm beginning to think maybe I did the wrong thing sending Eli out there."

"Mr. Trent, Eli was just the one to send. He and Houston make a good team. They both know what they're doing."

"If I lose my grandson," Trent said, "you want to try telling that to Mrs. Trent?"

Masterson understood. "We'll stay on it, Mr. Trent"—he turned to leave—"and we'll let you know the instant anything comes in."

"Thank you." Trent sat, looking weary. "I know you will."

CHAPTER 19

The beam from Mark's pistol struck the poised tentacle a few inches back of the point where it divided. The tentacle parted, whipping and jerking like a fire hose, spraying greasy fluid in every direction. The cable around Carole's body tightened. Mark ran to her and grabbed at the coils, but they slid around her, clamping her even more securely. He realized they would kill her if they continued to squeeze.

Backing away, he aimed the pistol at the base of the table where the cable began to thicken and fired. As the coils loosened and dropped to the floor, the mound in the middle of the room emitted strange pig-like squeals. Mark scooped Carole off the table and ran, carrying her to the side of the room.

He put Carole down against the wall. Carefully he targeted the ten-foot mass in the center of the room and pulled the trigger. The beam dug into its middle, causing the mound to smoke and quiver. In the next instant, everything stopped; the entire hall became silent. Mark turned to retrieve Caro—

KABOOM!

The lights went out as the mound exploded. A wave of concussion from the blast knocked him into the wall beside Carole. The side of his head struck the thick steel plates, and a white flash popped inside his eyes. He became dizzy and his legs weakened as he struggled against losing consciousness. Unable to remain standing, he dropped to his knees and shook his head several times, fighting the blackness away. With a tremendous effort, he pushed himself up along the wall.

The remains of the monstrous machine were burning. Acrid-smelling smoke and dust filled the room. Most of the tables were overturned, and many of the people had been thrown to the floor. None moved.

He felt a sharp pain and tried to move his arm, but it would not respond. The source of his distress, he saw, was a sliver of wood twice as thick as a pencil imbedded in his left shoulder. Four inches of the sliver protruded. Mark felt a wave of weakness and fell back against the wall.

He switched on his flashlight. Stabbing the beam through the semi-darkness, he saw Carole lying a few feet away. He switched off the light and put it in his back pocket, then went to her. He pulled her onto his back, hitching her up so that she was balanced over this right shoulder. He looked for his gun, but he couldn't see it in the flickering light and choking haze. *Right now, getting out of this place is more important.* He gave up on the gun and began to make his way back toward the entry.

He edged along the wall, stepping over crumpled bodies.

Sweat poured off him as the ache in his shoulder became almost unbearable. His heart pounded, his legs shook, and he couldn't catch his breath. Certain he was not going to make it any further, he stopped, then struggled to gather what strength he had left. He forced himself to inhale to the full capacity of his lungs and again pushed himself along the wall, fighting against the weakness and nausea. The dust, smoke, and pain were too much, he was sure. He lifted his head one last time to try to see through the hazy air. A few yards ahead was the doorway.

I can't make it. My God, I'm going to die here, in this devilish place, millions of miles from ho—

"No!" he shouted with a snarl. "Not yet, dammit!"

He repositioned his burden and, despite the overwhelming pain, edged his way to the door. Leaning against the frame, he worked the pad and watched the door slide open. Almost at the point of losing consciousness, he dumped Carole's limp form into the room beyond. He followed, almost falling himself, then reached back and punched the pad. The door slid shut.

Darkness and quiet enveloped them.

Exhausted and unable to resist further, Mark slumped to the floor and lapsed into senselessness.

CHAPTER 20

On the drive home, Draper kept thinking about Hawthorne and all the times he had seen this little brown mass but never done anything about it. In fact, he had continually dismissed it as insignificant. Not until Draper called his attention to it was he even interested in checking out the physical characteristics of the mass.

He wheeled into the driveway and exited his car, noting that it was almost seven o'clock. Walking to the house, he saw his wife Debbie through the window, sitting on the couch watching television. She was lounging barefooted in Levi's and one of his plaid shirts.

"God, what a good-looking woman you are," he said *sotto voce* as he closed the door.

"Hi, honey." Smiling, she got up from the couch to greet him. "How'd it go today?"

"All in all, not bad." He gathered her in and kissed her full. She uttered a lilting laugh and broke away.

He hung his jacket on the coat tree near the front door and walked into the living room where he picked up the newspaper from the coffee table and sat down in the big, overstuffed lounge chair. She began mixing him a Manhattan, telling him she'd made pasta fagioli. The dish, an old world Italian favorite of his Debbie had learned from her mother, featured cannellini beans.

"I chopped up some onions for you, too. Are you hungry?" She knew he liked to spread pieces of fresh onion on top of his pasta fagioli.

"Sure am," he said, his mouth watering. "Have I ever told you how wonderful you are?"

She grinned. "Sure, for your belly." She brought him his drink. "Here. I'll get you some dinner." As she moved toward the kitchen, he glanced through the newspaper.

Other than the usual stories about a couple of muggings and one drug-related murder downtown, he saw nothing particularly interesting. He was about to put the paper down when he spotted and article on the front page of the metropolitan section about Trent Enterprises and its attempts to discover what had happened to its two cargo ships that had mysteriously disappeared. The report went into some detail including the fact that Carl Trent's grandson Eli and Mark Houston were investigating. The thrust of the article was toward the economic difficulties Trent might have as a result of the lost cargo and other related expenses. Another item reported the death of Pollie Houston at Kensington Hospital. He noted that although the collision with the building was mentioned as the cause, nothing else of significance was written about the incident. The deputy sheriff was not mentioned.

Again he thought about the curious tumor. He became more determined than ever to discover what it was all about. He smiled at the notion that the tumor had become a distraction.

Debbie called to him from the dining room. He finished his drink and went in, seeing with pleasure that she had added some garlic bread to the serving.

"Thanks, honey, that smells great," he said as he sat down.

She sat across from him, a small glass of wine in hand. "I've already eaten"—she reached over and picked up a piece of the crunchy golden bread—"but I'll join you for this." She noticed his frown. "What's bothering you, honey?"

"Well, it's interesting. I'm trying to figure out something about a little mass, like a tumor, that has been showing up in a few people's heads during autopsies. The thing is, the mass doesn't seem to have affected their health, but it's very unusual: it's too heavy for its size, it can't be cut, and when we tried to see inside it, nothing was there."

"What! That sounds impossible. Why can't it be cut?"

While he ate, he related most of what he had been doing. When he finished, his wife's face revealed further puzzlement.

"How many of these things have you seen?" She began to gather up the dishes.

"Let me help you." He picked up the deep dish and his fork and spoon. "I've only seen one, myself," he said, "but I've checked on half a dozen or them through various records and over a period of almost fifteen years. What I can't figure out is why Reggie has never been concerned about them. He acted as if they were nothing because he thinks there's no apparent connection between these people's deaths and this little brown chunk of stuff."

"Do you think there's a connection?"

"I have no reason to—yet—but some things just don't fit."

"Well, honey, maybe Doctor Hawthorne's just been too busy to follow up on it. You feel like some dessert?"

"What do you have?"

She reached inside the refrigerator and brought out a large wicker bowl of apples, peaches, pears, and plums, and put the bowl on the kitchen table.

Draper sat looking the fruit over. Finally he selected a juicy-looking plum and bit a big piece out of it. Liquid ran down his chin.

"Slob," she said, laughing. She tore a paper towel off the rack and handed it to him.

"Thanks, honey. What just doesn't make sense is that if I ran into something like this mass, I couldn't rest until I found out what it was."

"That's obvious," she said. "Have you talked to Mark Houston? Maybe he knows something about all this."

"No, I haven't. I left word for him to contact me, though. He doesn't even know his wife is dead."

"My God. Don't you think you ought to tell him what you found on the autopsy? He's entitled to know, isn't he?"

"Absolutely. I just haven't heard anything from him."

Having finished fitting the dishes in the dishwasher, she

started the machine and left the kitchen. At the bottom of the stairs, with a foot on the first step, she paused.

He saw her standing, silent.

"What?"

"Greg, is it possible Doctor Hawthorne is doing some kind of experimenting?"

"Reggie, I have a couple more questions about that mass you found in Mrs. Houston's head. What's your schedule like this afternoon?" Draper was calling from his own office after completing his routine for the morning.

"What now, Greg? I thought I gave you everything I had."

"Well, I guess you did at the time, but a couple of things have come to light since. Can I meet you in your office, say, around two?"

"Well, let me see . . . Sure, I can be free for a while."

Draper thanked him and hung up, his emotions mixed.

Somehow, this whole situation seemed more than a little bizarre.

CHAPTER 21

Mark lay stretched out on his back. He opened his eyes but saw nothing. He blinked. Still total blackness.

I'm dead.

The enormity of the presumption sent a chill through his body, but the sharp pain in his shoulder and his sweat-soaked clothing brought another conclusion: *I'm blind.*

This idea, too, was frightening. He could not remember what might have caused the event, and he knew if he could not see, his position would be perilous.

He brought his right hand to his left shoulder and touched the piece of wood protruding from it. He grunted as millions of needles jumped from the spot and spread into his chest . . . It all came back. *We're outside that damned room, and I'm not blind. It's just the darkness. Calm down.*

He forced himself to breathe evenly.

Gathering what strength he could, Mark pushed off the

floor with his good arm and sat up. He felt himself getting dizzy, but he shook his head and fought it off. He rubbed his eyes with his hand but still saw nothing. Then he became aware of the heat.

It must be a hundred degrees in here. What the hell's going on?

He leaned forward and searched with his right hand in small arcs on the thinly carpeted floor. Aware by a sixth sense that something was just beyond his fingertips, he stopped. Alert and cautious, he walked his hand like a spider, his skin supersensitive for the tiniest contact. His fingertip touched a soft surface. Another finger contacted the object—skin—Carole's skin.

Her body was warm and sweating, like his own. She was on her side with her back to him and her head near his feet. As he edged closer, he could hear her slow breathing. He followed the contours of her body with his hand until her reached her shoulder and shook her gently.

"Carole?"

No response.

He could not remember if she'd been injured by the blast inside the hall. His attention had been strictly on getting them out of that place alive.

The flashlight. It must be close by.

He again slid his hand around the floor. Behind him and to his right, his fingers found and closed around the tubular casing. Mark pressed the on switch. The light was so bright that at first it made him squint.

The space, a sort of anteroom or hallway, was devoid of furniture. It looked to be about forty feet long and ten feet wide. On the walls and some computer panels were a few posters. Only the door openers at each end were lit.

He moved the beam to his right and illuminated Carole. He grasped her shoulder, pulling her onto her back. No injuries or wounds were visible.

He stopped.

She lay stretched out, nude, in front of him—this woman with whom he had been intimate and in love for more than ten years. Some minutes before, he had risked his life for her and never given it a second thought. She had been in extreme danger, and he now realized that he never considered what might have happened to him or anyone else when he made his move. In the instant, he'd simply done what was required—to save her. *Somehow, the Fates, or God, or whoever has brought us back together. I can't stop the way I feel about you, and I wouldn't if I could. We're going to make it right this time.*

She could have been sleeping. She was tantalizing and beautiful and desirable. The contours of her small, firm breasts blended down her ribs into her flat stomach. Her left leg was straight and her right formed a triangle with it, her foot resting flat against her left shin. Her thighs were apart, and his point of view was from just above her knees. Her body was smooth and sleek with perspiration, except for a small tuft of dark fur that rose just below her abdomen.

He shook his head. *What a beautiful creature you are.*

Picking up the light, he turned it onto his own shoulder. The idea of pulling the splinter out occurred to him, but he rejected it. *The wound will probably start to bleed again.* He could feel the point apparently rubbing on the bone. Although the entry point hurt, what alarmed him was that his left middle and index fingers felt numb. *The thing apparently cut some nerves.*

Mark flexed the fingers of his left hand. Though they worked, he felt some tingling and loss of sensitivity. He moved the arm, but the pain prevented full use. He had strength, but it wasn't normal.

He put the flashlight back on the floor, pointed up. It reflected off the white ceiling and made it possible to see the entire room, although it was only a bright shade of gray.

Reaching for Carole's face, Mark palmed her chin and shook her head, calling to her.

She opened her eyes and looked up at him. "Mark," she said in groggy surprise. Pulling herself up to lean on her elbows, she asked, "What's happened? . . . Where are we?"

"We're on Geneva Station and in a lot of trouble. What happened to you? Are you hurt?"

She sat up, looked down at her body, then crossed her arms in front of her. "I'm okay. Where are my clothes?"

"I haven't any idea. It was just dumb luck I found you. The only reason I ended up here is that I was trying to find out what happened to the engineering functions for the station so I could light the place and maybe have a better chance of finding you. Well, I found you as your are, inside the hall of the other side of this door. Hundreds of people, all naked, were held down to tables. They seemed to be in a trance. A damned monster machine was about to perform some kind of weird operation on you. When I saw it was you, I couldn't believe it. This big tubular arm was hovering over you. I saw it injecting something into a woman just before you, and it was going to do the same to you, so I blasted the machine the arm was attached to. I didn't realize the machine would blow up. It made a helluva mess—including this." He pointed to his shoulder.

"How bad is it?"

"Well, it hurts." He looked down at his left shoulder. "The sliver is all the way to the bone, and I can't use my left arm much, but I'm afraid I'll live. Look, I don't know how long we've been here, but I sure as hell don't want to have another run-in with that—whatever that damned thing is. Apparently, buddies of his are spotted around out there."

He told her what followed and summarized what had happened since she disappeared at the airlock door. "So what the hell happened to you?"

"I don't know," she said. "All I remember is I was standing at the airlock door. Before I could yell or do anything, my head was wrapped with something that felt like a huge snake. The thing picked me up, and the last thing I remember, I was being smothered. I thought that was it. I passed out. Next think I know, I'm here with you. What happened to the rest of the people inside?"

"After that explosion and fire, I don't think anybody's left."

Carole picked up the flashlight. "We'd better find out." She looked at him, her face determined.

"God, what do you expect to do?" His voice rose a level or two in exasperation. "I told you, the place was on *fire*. We can't go back in there. Look, Carole, this whole place keeps getting hotter, and I have a feeling that if we don't get out of here soon, we're going to get baked."

"Your said you destroyed the machine, didn't you? We've got to check, Mark. If anyone's left, they'll need our help."

She was right, he knew. "Okay, help me get this shirt off—at least you can put it on." He stood and began to unbutton it.

"No, never mind—unless you want me to take that thing out of your shoulder. What's the difference? I'm not cold."

He managed a half smile. "Okay. Let's go."

They helped each other to stand and made their way to the door. At the computer pad, she turned to him.

"Ready?"

"You're crazy, you know. Okay—do it."

CHAPTER 22

The smoke and dust in the great hall had mostly settled, but a few small fires lingered, lending an eerie bouncing yellow light to the place. Bodies were strewn everywhere.

As Mark and Carole crept about inside, they recognized only one person in the immediate area: Jim Conroy, the engineer.

"Oh, Jesus," Mark said.

Conroy was dead, having been torn almost in two.

"Mark, I've known Jim for almost a year. He was a good man. What I want to know is, how the hell did he get here? He left with Karen—Doctor Bradley. She must be here, too."

"Most of the women were over on the far side, where I saw you." He pointed across the hall. "Over there."

The had only gone a few steps when she pulled at this arm. He turned to look at her, and she put her index finger to her lips.

Mark listened, but heard nothing.

"Look," she whispered, pointing across the room.

A small glowing sphere, about the size of a softball, was darting a few inches above the

smoking ruins. Lit from within and pulsating in various shades of beige and brown, the sphere was emitting a soft, high-pitched whine.

Carole and Mark dropped behind a table that had been knocked on its side. They watched, fascinated, as the object bounced and stopped over bits of wreckage, avoiding places where fires still burned. Whenever it paused, the pulsing increased, and it emitted that soft squealing sound.

"The sphere seemed to come out of the wall, there, in the middle," Carole whispered, indicating a small opening in the center of the opposite wall. "Where's the gun?"

"I lost it during the explosion. It must be somewhere along that wall. I was trying to get you our of here after all hell broke loose." Mark looked back to the right, trying to recall where they had been. "Stay here. I'll see if I can find it."

Her grasp tightened twice in succession on his hand.

He froze. The object was coming across the room at them.

Carole was behind the tabletop, her hands on the edge, the upper half of her face above the edge. She seemed spellbound and didn't move.

The sphere stopped less than a yard away, a little above their eye level.

Mark inched back against the wall, a few feet behind Carole.

The ball's vivid surface shifted and flowed like muddy

water. The ball remained floating but began to make small noises in dozens of frequencies all at once and became brighter, almost yellow.

Mark's stomach tightened. He moved to his right. Seeing no reaction from the sphere, he crept a few more feet. He grew confident that the sphere was some kind of sensing device apparently capable of investigating only one entity at a time. He slipped behind a tangle of debris and bodies and glanced back at the scene.

The sphere had drifted closer to Carole's face. She remained unmoving, her eyes wide, staring directly at the strange ball, now less than a foot from her face.

Mark continued to search for the hammer gun. He crawled toward the spot where they were standing when he fired on the machine. He was sure the gun was buried somewhere close by and began to pick his way through the mass of remains and wreckage.

He spotted the hammer gun's handle under a dead woman's thigh. He grabbed the weapon at the same instant that he heard Carole give a small moan. "Down!" he shouted. In one motion, he spun around and pulled the trigger."

Carole's head disappeared below the edge of the table just as the beam impacted the quivering globe with a white flash accompanied by the loud shattering of crystal. Bits of debris flew in all directions.

Seconds passed. Mark remained in shooting position, waiting, his mind picturing Carole crouching, probably injured by the pieces of the exploding object.

Her fingers appeared on the edge of the table, follow by her face. She was grinning. *"Nice* shot."

CHAPTER 23

When the police arrived at St. James Hospital just after one in the afternoon, three of them were escorted by a frightened nurse to Doctor Hawthorne's third floor office.

As they neared, the nurse began to tremble. She would not enter. They pushed past her and went inside.

Blood covered almost the entire floor. Something that appeared to be a half-eaten animal occupied the top of the desk. Streams of blood dripped from the carcass onto the white tile. Various surgical instruments were scattered about the room. The air was laden with the pungent odor of exposed internal body organs. Sgt. John Franklin, a street-wise hulk of a man with sixteen years on the force, went in and approached the desk, trying to avoid stepping in blood. The look on his face changed from curiosity to abject horror.

The grotesque remains of a human being had been carved, chopped, and dismembered. What remained was an armless, legless, nude torso with the head of a woman whose stomach cavity was empty.

Sergeant Franklin felt a great wave of nausea. As he turned toward the door, he saw a slumped figure behind it. His eyes widened as he contemplated the man whose own stomach was a huge balloon and whose lower body was completely red with blood, some of which had emanated from his mouth.

Franklin stepped closer to the body and reached down to lift the chin of Dr. Reginald Hawthorne. When he did, the body fell sideways away from the door. The doctor's right arm was partially buried in a large vertical cut in his side.

Cautiously, the officer gripped the dead man's forearm just below the elbow and began to pull it out. Something seemed to be blocking it, so Franklin tugged on the arm. With an audible slurp, Hawthorne's hand slipped out of his bloody corpse. Within the grasp of his dead fist was a large scalpel that, as the instrument came free, easily parted the wall of the doctor's upper abdomen from the inside.

Folds of flesh fell back from the gaping wound. Franklin watched, spellbound, as seven bloody fragments spilled out onto the floor. He recognized some as human fingers and toes, the nails of which were covered with a light pink polish.

Shocked beyond anything he had ever experienced, Franklin could not move. The nausea began anew in huge, uncontrollable undulations. He tasted the acidity as it rushed up from his stomach.

Hearing his partner retching, the second younger officer stepped inside the room. "John, what—" He peered behind the door, and his face paled. "Oh, sweet Jesus!"

Just inside the St. James Hospital staff entry, two nurses and three interns were sitting on hall benches, arms wrapped around one another. One of the nurses was being interviewed by a uniformed policewoman.

Hearing someone enter, one of the male interns looked up. He recognized the man and hurried to him. "Doctor Draper! Oh, God, Doctor Hawthorne is dead."

"What! What happened?"

"I don't know." The intern's eyes were wide, and he spoke quickly. "I mean, we just heard about it. Laurie found him, and she's been crying and hysterical ever since. The cops are up there now. His office looks like a slaughterhouse. Christ, I've never seen anything like it. There's blood all over the place."

"Wait a second—slow down. Where did this happen?"

"In his office, Doctor. They found a woman's body all cut up on top of his desk, and he was behind the do—"

"Okay, okay, try to take it easy." Draper steered the intern toward the group and strode toward the elevator. At its doors, he identified himself to police and went up.

When he exited the elevator, he almost bumped into two more police officers. He identified himself again and walked down the hall toward Hawthorne's office where a small crowd were talking and making notes.

As he approached with ID badge in hand, Draper noticed some red footprints outside the door. Before he could get close enough to see into the office, a tall wiry man of about fifty with craggy looks and a full head of short white hair stopped him. The man shifted the old brown suit he wore, introduced himself as Detective Lieutenant Dick Freeman, and inspected Draper's credential. He inquired as to what the doctor wanted.

"Doctor Hawthorne was a friend of mine," Draper explained. "Can you tell me what happened?"

Without responding to his question, Lt. Freeman invited hm into an adjoining office where they sat down. It appeared, he said, that Doctor Hawthorne had killed the woman, stripped her, and then chopped her into pieces. "From what I can gather, it looks like he wanted to cannibalize her. It's pretty gruesome, Doctor Draper. Do you have any idea why he would have done this?"

"Good God, no. I've known him for years, Lieutenant. There's no reason for anything like this. Who was the woman?"

"One of the nursing staff. We're trying to find out if there was any kind of relationship between them."

"I don't think so. Reggie was a genuine family man. He has a wife and two kids, and he loves them dearly. I think I would have known if he were fooling around."

"Well, maybe. Sometimes you'd be surprised at what your friends are really like. I mean, think about it, Doc. Do you ever put the same face on at the hospital that you wear at home? Anyway, we're checking everything out."

Draper wanted to look into Hawthorne's office, but the yellow "Crime Scene—Do Not Cross" tape prevented him from seeing more than the bloody desk.

The detective took his telephone number and gave him his business card, telling him he would probably want to talk with him again. "You can go now, Doctor Draper."

CHAPTER 24

On his way home, Draper's thoughts wandered to when he and Hawthorne worked together a few years before. One autumn evening, a terrible collision occurred between a fuel truck and a bus full of kids returning from a football game. The accident took the lives of several children and severely injured and burned many others. The emergency room was a nightmare as the two of them worked into the early morning hours. The truck driver and one schoolgirl nearly died on the table—and might well have it if hadn't been for the dedication and skill of Reggie Hawthorne. He demonstrated again and again that he could always be counted on when the chips were down. Draper felt sad, angry, and frustrated.

He parked his car in the driveway and went to the front porch where he bent down and picked up the newspaper. The headline caught his eye: *Series of Bizarre Killings Baffle Police.*

The story began with a graphic description of Hawthorne's death, including some details that Lieutenant Freeman had not shared. The report stated that some of the body parts of the woman had been chewed off rather than cut. Reports of numerous other grisly murders in various parts of the country followed, all of which were tied together by the killer's having tried to eat the victim, and the crimes having happened *almost at the same moment.*

One incident occurred in Washington, D.C. where a rabbi— a friend of the vice president—killed his own wife and daughter. A neighbor found him sitting quietly at his dining room table, the dissected remains spread out like any ordinary meal.

Another event dealt with a couple in Pennsylvania. She had tried to consume most of his left arm. The woman calmly waited until the police arrived.

Each of those who were able to explain said they simply wanted to do what they had done. None of this made any sense to authorities who were appealing to the public for help in sharing any information that might be of assistance.

Studying the names, Draper saw none that were familiar except Hawthorne's. "Why all at the same time?" he wondered aloud as he opened the door to his home.

"Oh, Greg!" Debbie greeted him wide-eyed and frightened. "I just heard the news about Doctor Hawthorne. The TV reported hundreds of killings are happening all over the world. What's going on?"

"All over the world! Where?"

She pulled him into the living room. "It's on TV now. Story

after story—from almost everywhere. All sorts of people have been killed. It's horrible. They're turning into cannibals! Listen."

They stood a few feet from the wall screen and watched in silence as the reports came in. Las Vegas. Detroit. Miami. Rome. Paris. Some small towns in scattered parts of Europe and Asia. One in Beijing. Several in Australia. With some variations, they were essentially the same: someone had gone berserk, killing the nearest person with no apparent motive. The methods differed, from manual strangulation to beatings to knives or guns, but in every case, the killer tried to eat the victim. In Latvia, a wealthy woman killed and completely ingested her own baby, then was shot to death when her husband came upon the scene.

The general sense from the newscasters was that the perpetrators were trying to forestall what they viewed as a possible worldwide panic.

Kensington Hospital was on the edge of pandemonium. By late evening, more than a hundred dead human beings had been brought in by police and ambulance. Several corpses had been partially eaten and were missing limbs or other body parts. The decapitated body of a young man approximately twenty years of age arrived in a bloody bag, his head having been removed from his torso by a number of blows from a hatchet. Another victim, a middle-aged woman, came in with one arm torn off, several chunks having been bitten from the forearm. The police were unable to offer any sort of reasonable explanation.

In all his professional life, Doctor Draper had never seen anything like this. Perhaps it made the situation a bit more tolerable in that he saw all the reports but had not performed the actual autopsies himself. After the first three, he decided not to watch the tapes but instead only to read the write-ups. Although a few of the names were familiar, he felt a small sense of relief that he knew none of them personally—until the ninety-eighth autopsy. Reginald Hawthorne.

He stared silently at the unopened file in his hands, reading the name again and again.

He picked up the front cover, leafed past four pages of printed material, and pulled the holotape out of the back pocket. He bounced it lightly in his hand, trying to decide whether or not he really wanted to see it.

"Okay, Reggie." He dropped the tape into the player and switched it on.

Most of the information, under the circumstances, was unremarkable.

Hawthorne's body was in gruesome condition, and remarks were made concerning the grisly contents of his stomach. A little more than halfway through, Draper's expression changed to a frown. He reached over and froze the frame. He squinted as he bent closer to the screen.

Inside the left rear portion of Reginald Hawthorne's skull was a small brown mass, identical to the one he had examined at the Kensington Laboratory.

"All right," he muttered, "where did you pick that thing up?"

During the next hour, he ran through another thirty of the

previous autopsies, this time checking each of the tapes, stopping at the point where the brain was being examined. Almost all of the corpses had the same anomaly: the familiar brownish tumor, located in the left cortex, midway between the occipital and temporal lobes.

All these people with the strange lump in their head had to have something in common

that produced the phenomenon, Draper reasoned. The more he searched, however,

the more puzzled he became. Their medical histories bore no resemblance to one another: no common illnesses, no symptoms that could be traced to a single cause, no similar genetic factors. He knew that a spontaneous generation like this lump in hundreds, perhaps thousands of people from different areas and all walks of life in exactly the same spot in their brain was asking too much of coincidence.

There has to be something more, something I'm missing. Where did they get this thing? How long has it been going on? Hawthorne said something about having seen these lumps for nearly twenty years. It's not any known disease; maybe it's the result of some airborne spore, or exposure to some chemical, some kind of agent.

"How the hell do I check this out?" he asked aloud, feeling frustrated and exasperated. Draper closed the latest folder and threw it on the desktop. He noted the time—10:45 p.m.—and suddenly felt exhausted. *Go home,* he told himself. *It'll have to wait.*

He put on his jacket and grasped the doorknob to leave when an idea entered his tired brain. Walking back to his desk, he searched out a small notepad and scrawled a two-word note to himself, then slipped a piece of tape from the dispenser and stuck the note to the lampshade of his desk light. He turned out the light and left the office, intoning as he went out the door, "Forest for the trees, dummy."

In large block letters on the slip of yellow paper he'd written: O T H E R D O C T O R S.

CHAPTER 25

Mark and Carole painstakingly made their way across the room, checking as many of the naked broken bodies as they could. Two men and one woman from the *Traveler* were still alive, but they were all so severely injured that their deaths were certain. They made them as comfortable as possible, then continued the search.

One by one, they found the rest of the crew members, all dead except for Doctor Bradley and Rico Martinez. Doctor Bradley was unconscious and bleeding from a gash on her forehead after having been struck by flying debris. Rico's left leg had been torn off. He was delirious with pain and loss of blood. They could find no trace of Eli Trent.

Carole bent over Doctor Bradley and cleared most of the blood from her face. They needed her medical skills, so she kept patting her face and calling to her, trying to awaken her.

Mark knelt beside Rico. With each pump of his weakening heart, more of the big man's blood spilled onto the floor into an ever-growing pool. Unless he could stop the bleeding, Mark knew his friend would die. He made his decision. He stuck the gun in his waistband and wrapped his fingers around the piece of wood in his shoulder. He paused, drew a deep breath, then jerked the sliver out.

His yell made Carole start. She spun around to see what caused it.

Mark was pulling his shirt off over his head. She saw blood oozing from his shoulder wound. He grimaced with his own pain as he tried to stop Rico's bleeding. He placed one sleeve under his foot, and, with his good arm, was attempting to knot the other sleeve around the slippery stump of Rico's leg. The shirt slipped off.

Seeing his difficulty, Carole came to his side. She helped him secure the bandage tightly enough to stop the flow of blood. While they worked to complete the makeshift tourniquet, Martinez lapsed into unconsciousness.

"Rico," Mark said through clenched teeth, "you better not die, you son of a bitch. I just gave you the shirt off my back."

Carole glanced at him and couldn't suppress a grin.

"We have to do something for you, too," she said. "That wound is bleeding again."

"Carole," Mark said, "Eli left the *Sentinel* with Rico. We have to find out where he is." He looked at this shoulder injury. A slow trickle of blood was running down his chest. He covered it with his hand. "This'll be okay. It'll stop in a minute. How's Doctor Bradley? She's got to look at Rico, and we have to find Eli. Then we all have to get the hell out of here. This place is going to get too damned hot."

Carole went back to check on the doctor, and Mark looked down at Rico. A wave of anxiety wash over him as he feared his old friend would not survive. He wanted to find something to cover him; his lying there, naked and mutilated, seemed obscene. Mark bent closer, trying to will Rico's body to fight. Heavy drops of sweat ran down his face and fell onto Rico's damaged body. Rico opened his eyes.

"Rico, come on, buddy. We've got to get out of here, all of us. Man, we have a lot of catching up to do, and there's some cold beer waiting for us. Where the hell is Eli, anyway? What happened to you guys?" As he spoke, Rico mumbled, and Mark reached for his big hand, which enclosed his own in a powerful grip. "Rico, I can't hear you. Talk to me. What happened? Where's Eli?"

"We were caught . . . in . . . some kind of beam . . . that pulled us down . . . We tried to"—he coughed and winced in pain—"we tried to get away from it . . . We couldn't. As soon as we got inside, some kind of big cables grabbed us. They were like snakes, man . . . They were alive . . . Oh, Jesus, Mark. My leg hurts . . . really bad." He drew a couple of deep breaths.

Mark held his head, making sure he could not see his legs. "You're going to be all right, Rico," he said. "What about Eli?"

"I don't know where Eli is . . ."

Carole helped Doctor Bradley to her feet, and they joined the two men. While the doctor hovered over him, Rico looked the two women over, then glanced toward Mark, a small smile crossing his lips. "Never saw them like that before."

Mark grinned, then his expression turned serious again.

"Look, my friend, we have to get off Geneva Station. It's been heating up steadily for the last couple of hours, and it must be well over a hundred degrees by now. I know you're hurting, but we've got to go."

"He's in bad shape," Bradley said. "He's lost a lot of blood, but I don't see any alternative, if things are as you say. All you have is the escape module, right? How are we all going to get in one of those?"

Carole turned to Rico. "Where's your EM?"

He explained that his vehicle was located near the middle of the central loading tube. That meant it was about two miles above them and perhaps a half mile from their module.

"Come on, we'd better get going," Carole said. "After we get Rico and Doctor Bradley to the shuttle, you and I will get back to the module. We're all going to have to sleep back to Earth Zone."

"Just a second," Mark said. "We've got to find Eli."

"And just where do you propose we start looking for him? We haven't any idea—" She pointed at another of the strange spheres moving across the hall. It paused over the wreckage of the machine in the middle of the room.

Mark took careful aim and fired. The globe disappeared accompanied by tinkling glass. His second shot struck the side of the opening from which it had emerged, and a muffled explosion followed. The hole appeared to be sealed shut.

"All right," Mark said, "let's move."

CHAPTER 26

Carl Trent's face showed the toll of the last two days. He had lost weight, and bags appeared under his eyes. His movements were slow and measured.

"Mr. Trent," Masterson began, "we're still trying to contact Geneva. So far, the station has not responded, but we have picked up the signal from the *Sentinel's* buoy. It looks like the *Sentinel* broke up, and indications are that everyone got out in their escape shuttles."

"What do you mean, 'broke up'?"

"Well, they haven't figured it all out yet, but I'll let you know as soon as we have more information. All we know is that Banning launched the autolog just before they abandoned ship."

"What about my grandson?"

"They're probably all on Geneva, sir. The only other possibility is that they decided to head home and sleep, but no ships have been spotted on such a track. I'm afraid that's all we have right now."

"Okay, Ed . . . Jesus, this is crazy. What the hell is going on out there?"

"I wish I knew, Mr. Trent. We've got a lot of people, two ships, and the ships' cargo missing, and not a clue as to why. The *Vikinghaul* and the *Monitor* are only a couple of hours away, so we've sent them to follow up. The *Vikinghaul* is empty of cargo and was on its way to Geneva for a routine pickup. The *Monitor* is one of the regular traffic vessels, the same class as the *Sentinel*."

Trent stepped over to the wet bar. "Would you like a drink?"

"No, thanks, Mr. Trent. I appreciate the offer, though, and I may take you up on that later."

Trent took a large snifter and a bottle of twelve-year-old brandy from the cabinet. He poured several ounces into the big glass.

"Look, Mr. Trent," Masterson said, "I know Eli, and I know Mark. They have their heads on straight, and I'm sure they're all right. Try not to worry too much, sir."

Trent took a large sip of his drink. "Yeah, Ed," he said. "Thank you."

The hot muggy darkness swallowed the foursome as they climbed through the exit. Carole, flashlight in hand, led them, while Mark and Doctor Bradley struggled with Rico. All dripped with sweat.

In the outer engineering spaces, they came upon a series of lockers along a wall. Bradley opened one and call to the group, "Well, look what we have here. Thank God!"

Inside each of the lockers were coveralls and lined boots. Obviously meant for colder conditions, the clothing was a fair compromise between their naked vulnerability and the excessive heat. They found sizes that roughly fit and climbed into them. Rummaging through the rest of the lockers, Mark discovered a worker's lunch pail in the bottom of one. He lifted the lid and was surprised to see a thermos full of coffee, no longer hot. He sniffed the coffee and was satisfied that it was drinkable. Whoever had left it had already added sugar and cream. "It's not a cold beer," he said, "but it's something to drink. Anybody want some?" The coffee was all his.

Outside the building, Mark passed the hammer gun to Carole so he and Bradley could help Rico. For the next half hour, they worked their way along the suspended walkways toward the central tube, pausing at intersections to decide their next move, always speaking in whispers.

"We've got to find one of the elevators," Mark said. "If we don't, we'll never make it."

"We'll make it," Carole said. "Elevators are all over the place. This whole station is designed to make it easy to get to the loading area in the middle. Just keep your eyes peeled for one of the info centers."

Rico's breathing was becoming labored, and Mark worried about how much blood he had lost. Mark was grateful that, as they progressed toward the station's center, gravity decreased making the burden of Rico's weight a little easier to handle.

Still, Mark felt a great sense of urgency. *If Rico's going to survive, we need to get him into one of the shuttles and put him into hibernation.*

At the next information center, they put the computer to work finding the elevators and located one less than a hundred yards further on.

As they were leaving the enclosure, Mark spotted four small lighted objects floating toward them from below. He nudged Carole and pointed them out. The objects were perhaps three hundred yards away and heading directly at them.

Carole trained her pistol on the nearest object. Her first shot missed by a few inches. The targets continued without varying their paths, but they increased their speed. Correcting her aim, she pulled the trigger again. As the yellow beam hit the leading globe, it exploded. The second globe, in a direct line immediately behind the first, collided with the debris from the first explosion and it, too, disintegrated.

Carole fired again, and the third ball was demolished—only fifty feet away. The last globe flew directly at Rico and the doctor and zipped between them. Carole swung the light on the pair. As the ball passed, it ejected two brown globs the size of golf balls at high speed, one toward each of them. Both were knocked aside, the bits slamming into their sides. Mark lost his footing, and all three dropped to the walkway. Rico, off balance and in pain, reached for the railing. His fingers brushed the cables, and he took another swipe. He missed and slipped off the walkway, one hand clamping onto its edge, his body dangling over the dark abyss.

After passing the group at terrific speed, the globe turned in a large arc. From two hundred feet away, it straightened its path and sped toward Carole. She fired twice, the second shot disintegrating the globe with less than twenty yards to spare.

Mark grabbed for Rico's wrist. The big man outweighed him, even in the lessened gravity, and because of the sweat on his hand and his weakened left arm, he realized he could not save his friend. Rico did not have the strength to hold onto the walkway. As his grip slipped to a finger-hold, he looked up at Mark. Carole jumped to their aid, but before she could help, Rico said, "It's okay, Mark," and released himself.

"NO!" Mark screamed. His heart pounded as, in horror, they watched Rico plummet out of sight without uttering a sound.

They turned to Karen Bradley. She was on her knees holding her side, gasping for air. Her face contorted and her eyes widened as she watched the expanding hole in her own right side. With blood flowing between her fingers, she tried to hold the gaping wound closed. She looked up at Mark and Carole with an expression of surprise. As Carole made a move toward her, the doctor coughed and pitched forward onto the walkway.

Carole crouched next to her. The grotesque hole in her side continued to expand, boiling and smoking. Doctor Bradley was dead.

Neither Mark nor Carole moved for a long moment. Mark felt fury building inside him like a liquid flame centered in his chest. The anger seemed to permeate every pore of his body, threatening to turn into an uncontrollable rage, a rage against an enemy that was mostly unseen, implacable, and outrageously diabolical. He felt at once helpless and impotent, and his mind began to tell him that struggling was useless and ridiculous, that he could never hope to get out alive, and that since he couldn't, he should do whatever was necessary to survive from one second to the next.

He breathed deeply and sighed before joining Carole who was still on one knee next to Bradley. Mark touched her shoulder. "We've got to get out of here," he said.

Together they walked toward the elevator. As they neared, the bouncing shaft of light revealed the door was open. They ran inside, exhausted, and fell against the back wall. As Mark reached out to touch the dimly-lit control panel, he became aware they were not alone.

Click!

A bright light struck them both in the face. A menacing voice behind the light announced, "I thought I might find you here. Don't move, or I'll kill you. I want you to know you are responsible for the deaths of nearly a million people," the voice in the elevator said. "And now, drop the gun."

"What the hell is going on, Eli?"

"I will kill you both right now if you don't put the gun down."

The pistol slid from Carole's hand onto the floor.

"I don't have time to explain," he said. "Just do what I tell you."

"Listen, you son-of-a-bitch, what's—"

"Shut up, Mark." Eli's voice had a frightening edge to it. "I told you I don't have time, and I mean it. We have to go." He touched the control pad, and, after the door closed, the elevator began a smooth, swift ride toward the center of the station. They rode in silence with Mark wondering how this man he had known all these years as a friend could suddenly turn on him. There had even been moments he might have considered Eli his closest friend. They had bellyached together more than once. Their laments were often bent on out-doing one another, particularly where the opposite sex was concerned, and Mark never felt his confidence had been misplaced.

Mark forced himself to calm down. He pondered ways to distract Eli so they could disarm him. He knew how difficult that would be since Eli could see them plainly, but they could not be sure where he was behind the blinding light. Even if they were able to evade that bright circle, they would be temporarily blind in the otherwise total darkness, so Mark decided to bide his time.

The elevator stopped, and Eli urged them out. They stepped into a workstation almost at the exact center of the loading area. Eli warned them to stay close as he opened the airlock door. A normal atmosphere had been restored to the tube. They emerged to see the six huge exhausts protruding from the tail end of a large cargo craft that was pointed away from the planet and toward the north doors.

"We're going for a ride," Eli said. He ordered them to move to the ship's side entry door. "Get aboard."

CHAPTER 27

Captain Mack Troyer of the *Vikinghaul* drew himself up as the ship neared the thin rings of Saturn. He watched the presentation on the fifteen-by-twenty-inch screen in

front of him for any sign of Geneva Station. The navigator began to call out the distance every few seconds and recommended decreases in speed, which Troyer duly ordered. When they were two thousand miles away, he saw the satellite as a large black dot against the background of the planet's surface. His ship was swinging in toward it on a long arc, so they would be entering at the station's away doors, a path he had taken many times before. Still, his communications officer informed him that ahead, no indications of life were evident— no lights or signals of any kind.

"We're coming up on the spot here the *Sentinel* explosion occurred. Scan for any kind of—"

"What's that small light near the side of the station?" Troyer asked.

"It's a ship, sir," Judy Nash said, "coming out of the away-side doors."

Almost as soon as it emerged, the ship turned away from them and sped off toward the far side of Saturn. The ship did not respond to their inquiry messages.

"Who the hell *is* that?" Troyer asked. "Why don't they answer us?"

"They might have everything turned off, Captain," Nash said, "or they could be on automatic."

"They'd still get our hail. If the ship is unmanned, we'd get the standard code. Something's very wrong here. Are they armed?"

"I get no indications on that. I'd say no. It's a cargo vessel, though it isn't as big as ours. We can probably catch them, sir. Shall we go after them?"

"Do it," he said. "A soon as we get them on our screens again, match their speed. Stay a couple hundred miles behind. Let's see what they're up to. Keep trying to contact Geneva, too, and let the company know what's going on."

They changed course to follow the mysterious vessel, watching as it continued on, apparently oblivious to the *Vikinghaul's* pursuit.

"Any luck with contacting Geneva?" Troyer asked.

"Nothing, sir," Nash replied.

"Alert Security," the captain ordered. "Have them prepare for possible confrontation. We might have some trouble here."

For twenty minutes, the other ship's course remained

unchanged as it continued to pull away from Saturn. Then Nash reported a slight turn in the other ship's direction.

"Plot a possible course for them and maintain our distance," Troyer said. "I'd like to know where they're going."

After another moment, the navigator said, "Sir, they seem to be headed toward Titan."

CHAPTER 28

As he sat tied into the communicator's chair with nylon bundling straps, Mark could only wonder what this was all about. Eli had said nothing since they left Geneva except to order them to move or stand or sit. Mark's shoulder continued to bother him, and he discovered he could hardly make any movement that did not cause pain.

Carole was seated on the floor bound tightly to a stanchion near the navigator's station. She watched silently as Eli moved quickly from place to place on the flight deck, making small corrections here and there, touching a pad or changing readings almost as though he were a robot.

"Eli," Mark said, "where are we going?"

Eli cracked a small smile. "We have an appointment," he said.

"Where? Who with?"

"Soon enough," he answered with a dismissive wave of his hand. "No more questions."

Apparently satisfied that the ship was on the correct course, Eli settled into the captain's chair. Mark continued to watch him for another few minutes, until Eli folded his arms on the console and dropped his head. He appeared to have fallen asleep.

Mark tried his bonds, hoping to work the cargo straps loose, but his efforts were futile. He glanced at Carole whose head was bowed onto her chest, her beathing slow and rhythmic. She, too, was sleeping. *For now, anyway, escape is impossible,* he realized. *I may was well get some rest myself.* He closed his eyes . . .

A small, reddish-yellow dot with a thin haze at its outermost edge drifted onto the screen. Eli, fresh from his nap, smiled as he made a small correction to the ship's path. "We're almost there," he announced.

"I should have figured that out," Carole said. "Titan's the only moon of Saturn that has any atmosphere."

"That's terrific. The only problem is," Mark said, "that atmosphere is almost one hundred percent nitrogen. We won't be able to breathe."

"You're both right," Eli said. "Don't worry, though. I have some conversion suits, so we can run around just as if we were back home. The suits take a little getting used to, but after a few minutes, you won't even notice."

"Conversion suits?" Carole asked.

"They developed them for us," Eli continued. "They have

no problem with the atmosphere the way it is, but they knew we would."

"Wait a second. Who the hell are 'they'?" Carole asked.

"I guess you could say they're a search party. They came here twenty-five years ago looking for some way to keep their war going. Their resources were pretty much exhausted, so they were looking for some of the stuff they need."

"What war?" she asked, her voice rising with frustration. "What 'stuff'?"

He waved them quiet again, but now Carole was having none of it. Her voice took on a strange, deadly edge. "Eli, nowhere is there a damned war. How the hell can a war be going on for twenty-five years and nobody's noticed? Are you nuts or what?"

"I have to get this thing landed," he said. "Shut your face. Now." The look he gave her was so menacing Mark thought he might kill her then and there. In silence, she slumped back.

Eli maneuvered the big ship toward the surface, setting down on the floor of a large rectangular depression the size of a football field. Surrounded by low hills dimly illuminated by the far-distant sun, the depression had a strange orange tint.

Eli shut the propulsion systems down, checked his prisoners' bonds, and without another word, left the bridge.

CHAPTER 29

The reactor core at the center of Geneva Station reached the point at which it could no longer maintain safe operation. Alarms in every compartment began to sound. The

central computer system took control of the emergency network, announcing in a

matter-of-fact female voice over the loudspeakers in every corner of the gigantic structure that the station was in imminent danger. Since no human response to the warnings had been noted in the allotted thirty seconds, the computer attempted to set procedures in motion intended to prevent any further deterioration of the situation. Even the heightened speed at which the messages were being sent along the thousands of miles of wiring was not fast enough.

In a tiny fraction of a millisecond, a flash of intense light and heat began at the very heart of Nuclear Reactor Number Two. Spreading instantaneously into a prodigious cloud of plasma with a temperature of nearly six million degrees, it took less than three seconds to vaporize the three hundred human bodies in the conference hall and the millions of tons of steel, fabric, and glass that had been that great monument to mankind's skill and ingenuity.

The *Vikinghaul* was well beyond the physical effects of the blast, but an alarm sounded when the intense light was detected by its sensors as a possible threat. The navigator notified Captain Troyer who punched up the view aft to see what was going on as his ship sped away just beyond Saturn's horizon. The outer edges of the huge blast were just visible, spreading out five hundred miles, where they rapidly yellowed and faded.

"Jesus, what the hell was that?" Troyer said.

"That had to be Geneva, sir," Nash said. "Somehow, the station has exploded."

Troyer gave a long sigh. "My God," he said, "this must be our lucky day."

Asleep on the lead ship, Eli Trent and his two passengers did not see the small flashing light on the panel of the navigator's empty position that canceled itself after twenty seconds.

Ed Masterson stood in front of Carl Trent's desk describing what he knew about the events of the last twenty-four hours. Trent sat stunned as Masterson shuffled through the folder of papers he had placed on Trent's desk, referring to them as he talked.

"It appears Geneva Station no longer exists, Mr. Trent," he

said. "Last night, the astronomers at Mount Palomar Observatory noticed what they say was an explosion at Geneva's exact position. After further checking, they are convinced it was nuclear—the reactors—so we can only conclude that Geneva blew up."

Trent leaned forward, his faced etched with an expression of deep pain. "Dear God," he said, "there were—what?—three hundred people there?"

"Three hundred twelve that we know about, sir. At least, that was the complement. Since we haven't had contact with the place for the last couple of weeks, we don't know for sure how many were actually there. Remember, though, everything we have indicates it was dark, and maybe no one was there at all.

"We had communications from the *Vikinghaul* just before the explosion," Masterson continued. "It seems they were chasing another ship that had just left Geneva. The other ship would not identify itself, but it was a large cargo vessel. A lot of people could have been on board, of course, but there's no way of knowing—they never answered *Vikinghaul's* hail. We're trying to see what ships logged into the area."

"Who is the *Vikinghaul's* skipper? Is that Troyer?"

"Yes, sir—Mack Troyer. They apparently went around behind Saturn just as Geneva exploded. Our last message from them came a few seconds before the explosion, and that's the last we've heard from them."

"And?"

"From what we can gather, sir, Captain Troyer had been trying to contact Geneva without any response. As the *Viking-*

haul approached to within a few hundred miles, this other ship took off from Geneva. Troyer intended to land on the station to try to find out what was going on, but when the other craft left, he decided to follow it. The other ship immediately turned away and accelerated toward the far side of the planet. Damn good thing they took off after it. Otherwise, they'd have gone up, too.

"Any word about my grandson—and Houston?"

"No, sir, nor any of the *Sentinel's* crew, either. The last we heard from them was when they abandoned the *Sentinel.* It's possible they're on the other ship. I hope so."

"What about the *Traveler* and the *Monitor*? Where are they?"

Masterson picked another sheet from the package. After scanning it for a moment, he said, "Nothing about the *Traveler. Monitor's* a few hours behind the *Vikinghaul*, Mr. Trent. At top speed, she'll be closing up fast. She's commanded by Pete Ekstrom, and I already brought him up to date. Here's the transcript if you want to see it."

"Okay. Good work, Ed. Anything else?"

"No, sir."

"All right. Keep me informed."

Masterson assured him he would, and added, "Try not to worry too much, Mr. Trent. Those guys know what they're doing."

"I hope you're right, Ed."

· · ·

"Well, that's where Geneva used to be." Captain Ekstrom pointed as the *Monitor* streaked past the position at four thousand miles above Saturn's colorful gaseous surface. "But there's no sign that Geneva Station was ever there—no debris, nothing. My God, millions of tons of satellite, gone. I just pray all those people got out of there."

No one else spoke.

"Kick 'er in the ass," Ekstrom said. "And update Trent. Let's get moving."

The *Monitor* sped on, following the path the *Vikinghaul* had taken.

CHAPTER 30

The list of doctors Gregory Draper compiled at first yielded little additional information. That morning he discovered fourteen who were responsible for coming up with causes of death in California, Arizona, and Nevada. Most had not seen anything unusual during their autopsies over the years. After two hours and many frustrating calls, Dr. Allen Sayer of Jason Memorial Burn Center in Las Vegas talked of the strange mass in the brains of a total of three people, one woman and two men.

"A middle-aged woman named Louise Eldridge was killed in a Las Vegas house fire about four years ago," Sayer told him.

A resident of Sacramento, Eldridge had been visiting an elderly friend on a particularly hot day in July. An electrical short in an air conditioning unit in her friend's home caused the fire. Both died, apparently of smoke inhalation.

"According to my file, the anomaly you're asking about

was found in Mrs. Eldridge's head and sent out to be examined, but I never received a report. Want me to check on it?"

"I'd appreciate that, Doctor Sayer. I'm trying to develop something here, and I need as much detail as you can get. What about the two men?"

"That was six months ago. I didn't personally perform those autopsies. I supervised my colleague, Catherine Meade, who performed the autopsies on the two men, brothers, who were found dead in the desert fifty miles east of the California-Nevada line. The cause of death was listed as dehydration and exposure. From what police could piece together, it seems the brothers took off from Vegas walking. I guess they figured they could cross the desert easily during spring. The write-ups indicate that a small brown tumor, believed to be benign, was found in the same place in the crania of both victims, but neither tumor was removed."

"Why not?"

"It doesn't say. But as I recall, Doctor Draper, nothing showed the tumors had anything to do with the men's deaths. I think Doctor Meade may have mentioned the tumor in passing, and I suppose she surmised the tumor was genetic since it was in both of them. Do you believe the tumors in the three of them were all caused by the same thing?"

"Well, I'm beginning to. Were the men residents of Nevada?"

Sayer paused. "No. They were from Ramona, California, a small town thirty miles east of San Diego. Oh—one other thing. I didn't take notice of this until just now, and I don't know if it has any bearing, but all the corpses have a small burn on their left nipple and a recent trauma to the left eye."

Draper raised one eyebrow. "You mean like a black eye?"

"Something like that, except the entire orbit was affected. Usually, if someone gets slugged, for example, only a portion —even a large portion but a portion—gets the familiar discoloration. These were complete, a full circle."

"What about the burns?"

"They were peculiar in that they appeared to be the result of an insertion of something like a hot needle, something that dug into the chest about seventy millimeters. The outer skin had been cauterized, but only a few millimeters deep."

He thanked Sayer and asked him to transmit the reports and anything else unusual he ran into.

His next conversation was with the chief of oncology in San Bernadino. Bernard Castle, a curmudgeon who had been in practice for almost fifty years, was at first reluctant to provide any information at all, particularly over the phone. Draper sold him by telling him to call the hospital to verify his credentials. After a few minutes, they were reconnected.

"This is Doctor Castle."

"Thank you for calling back," Draper said. "I'm doing some research, Doctor, and part of it has to do with the discovery of some possible effects from a small, apparently benign tumor that has been showing up in the brains of a number of patients."

After summarizing the kind of information he sought, Draper waited while Castle searched his records. Castle capsulated a number of them. Recording the information on an iPad,

Draper was surprised when Castle revealed that the latest two deaths, both by massive heart attacks, occurred in Las Vegas. Both were males in their eighties. In separate incidents, each had, without warning, viciously attacked innocent bystanders outside hotels. Each assailant fell to the sidewalk and, even in the throes of cardiac arrest, inflicted deep bite wounds on the legs of their victims. One of the old men broke his dentures in the effort.

"It was the most bizarre thing I'd ever seen," Castle said. "One of these old guys probably didn't weigh a hundred twenty pounds soaking wet, yet he beat holy hell out of a man twice his size—killed him. You figure those lumps in their brains had something to do with this?"

"I'm not sure," Draper said, "but it's beginning to look like it. Would you send me copies of those autopsies?"

"Sure, absolutely. Say, we have more autopsies from last night and yesterday. You want copies of them?"

"Yes, thank you, anything you think might help. I appreciate it." He gave Castle his fax number, saying he preferred the fax because of concerns about online security. "Did these men show anything else unusual?"

"Let me see . . . Yes. One of my assistants found that the left nipples of the men had almost been burned off."

"Burned off?"

"Yes. The left nipple of each man was burned almost to the point where it was no longer discernible."

"Really. And I'll be they both had contusions that covered the entire orbital area, left eye."

"That's right," Castle said. "How did you know?"

"It's beginning to fit a pattern," Draper said. "Thanks a lot, Doctor Castle. If anything interesting comes of all this, I'll let you know."

His brow furrowed, Draper replaced his cell in its case. "Las Vegas," he said aloud. "Always Las Vegas . . . and burns and black eyes." He got up from his chair, walked to the window, and looked at the bright-blue morning sky, stretching his mind toward the city of gambling in the middle of the desert.

Somebody or something was directly responsible for all these people's deaths, most likely some kind of electrical machine precisely controlled, he was convinced. *But why shock someone, and why with such severity that the skin is burned, cauterized? I'm sure that's to stop bleeding—but why? And why always the left side?*

In four of the reports, the patients died in the presence of other doctors who each stated that the person's eyes altered to dark brown or black just before the person expired, and the eye color did not return to normal, whatever that color was, until some minutes after death.

"What the hell," Draper said aloud. "Maybe it's the water."

CHAPTER 31

I just can't figure any of this out," Mark said, "unless these people, whoever they are, are after the theorium and Eli's involved with them. I could see, with his help, how they could get those two ships that disappeared. He could have easily disabled the autobuoys. Hell, he knows them inside out. That stuff would be worth an awful lot of money to Trent's competition, but what's all this talk about war? Nobody has to go to war over theorium. Fusion plants are already being built all over the world. It doesn't make sense."

"This whole damn thing is crazy," Carole said.

The main hatch opened. Eli walked in carrying three bulky black nylon bags that he threw on the floor. He slipped a hammer gun out of his belt, stepped over to Mark's position, and began to untie him, all the while carefully keeping the gun out of reach yet menacing him with it.

"Open one of those bags, take off your clothes, and get into the suit," Eli told them. "Be sure to open the valve on the chest plate after you slip the suit on. When you're finished, come back over here—and don't try to be a hero, Mark."

Mark got up as soon as his bonds were loosened. He followed Eli's directions, laying out the gray outfit from the bag. The garment appeared to be an ordinary, full-body jumpsuit including boots, with closures running the length of one side. Gloves were attached to the end of each sleeve. A large metallic plate covered the chest area. Some buttons were undefined. Also attached was what appeared to be a communicator of some sort.

"They're designed to contact as much of the body as possible so the sensors can monitor your oxygen needs," Eli explained. "I wouldn't want you to pass out while we're outside. Be sure the zips are sealed, then put the helmet on. Your first breath will start the air flowing."

Mark struggled into the suit, running his fingers over the closures that stuck together firmly at his touch. The inside was lined with a thin, white, felt-like material, under which he could feel tiny tubes pressing against his entire body, even his fingers and toes. He picked up the helmet—a lightweight, clear plastic bubble—and put it on, making the quarter turn to lock it in position.

As he inhaled, the material seemed to come alive, hugging his form. For an instant, he panicked. When he let out his breath, he heard a tiny hissing as the atmosphere inside adjusted to his metabolism. He relaxed, and Eli waved him back to his former position, whereupon he tied him up again.

Loosening Carole, Eli cautioned her, "Don't do anything stupid."

"I understand." She smiled slightly at him and moved toward the second bag. Opening it, she spread the suit on the floor.

As Mark watched, he realized she was making every motion as seductive and sexual as she could. She stood facing Eli, waiting, while he took in her nakedness with his eyes.

"Nice try, Carole." He pointed the pistol directly at her stomach. He was smiling, but his tone was even. "You're a very desirable woman, but I don't have time for that right now. Maybe I'll take you up on it later. Now hurry up and get into the suit."

Her smile faded as she complied.

Eli secured her to the post again, then stripped and donned the third outfit. When he made sure all the suits functioned properly, he freed his captives once more. Cautiously he moved them out of the bridge, through the ship, toward the barren surface of Titan. "Stop at the bottom of the ramp, and don't move," Eli ordered.

With the glow of the ship's interior lights behind them, Mark and Carole dutifully obeyed, stepping into the Titan night. Mark's mind raced, taking in the surroundings, trying to see a way to get the upper hand. Without a weapon, he realized overcoming Eli was almost futile, unless he could get him to approach them closely enough to disarm him. Mark looked at Carole, who stood quite still, staring straight ahead.

Eli touched the keypad just inside the exit door. Light flooded the area from three large slots just above the opening.

Almost the entire half of the valley was illuminated, a flat plain of mottled orange, black, red, and gray. Stepping down to the surface, Eli walked a few paces to their left. From a pocket of his attire, he produced a small metallic box, pointed it toward a spot a few yards in front of them, and pressed the top with his thumb.

A rectangular section twenty feet across began to open in the ground. As it lifted, a brilliant yellow glare spewed out, many times brighter than the light from the ship. When it reached vertical, it stopped, its shiny underside facing them like a gigantic mirror. Beneath it was a square hole, ten feet deep. After another touch on his control, a platform rose from below. In the middle of the platform was a block of what appeared to be brown glass, about six feet square. At its center was a doorway.

"All right, let's go," Eli ordered, waving them forward. "Inside."

Carole and Mark followed a staircase down another thirty feet to where the stairway ended exactly in the center of a circle of smooth black floor ten feet in diameter. Directly ahead was a tunnel, just high enough for them to walk through upright. Its curved walls were also black with a thin, glowing, white horizontal line halfway up its sides. Mark felt a small twinge of claustrophobia.

"I'm right behind you," Eli reminded them. "Go ahead."

A few yards inside, the route turned to the right, then straightened again for a dozen or so paces. To Mark, it appeared to be a dead end, but as they came nearer, they realized they were in front of a tightly-sealed double door. Carole came up alongside Mark clutching his forearm. He turned, and as their eyes met, he saw fear in hers.

Eli again manipulated his little box. The split ahead of them widened, and they were confronted by a second set of closed doors. Eli urged them into the small square anteroom, and the first doors hissed shut behind them. Although it was not as dark, Mark was reminded of the encounter with Eli in the elevator on Geneva Station, which was roughly the same size.

"You can remove the helmets now," Elie said, taking his own off and setting it on the floor. Mark and Carole did the same. They inhaled clean, cool air that seemed to be the same as that of the atmosphere on Earth.

"Considerate of your friends to provide an airlock," Carole said.

"Tell her yourself." Eli opened the second set of doors.

They stepped into a cavernous dome-shaped chamber roughly hewn out of the planet's varicolored rock. The chamber was lit in the same manner as the tunnel—a bright band imbedded in the total circumference, a few feet up from the shiny black floor. In the middle of the space was a great silvery-brown mass nearly forty feet high, shifting and quivering with an ominous, dreadful energy. The mass was a larger rendition of the others Mark had seen. Revolving in slow tight circles around the creature were two dozen small glowing orbs. Mark recognized them as the same kind of globes that had killed Rico and Doctor Bradley.

CHAPTER 32

The approaching twilight brought the sun's rays directly into the outside rear mirror as Doctor Draper drove the lonely road eastward toward the desert. Shifting his position to move out of the reflected glare, he relaxed the pressure on the accelerator reducing his speed to seventy, while his vision adjusted to the highway scene ahead.

Throughout the three hours since he left San Diego, his mind had been occupied with the unusual events of the last two days. He had no clear idea what he was looking for, but he was certain that the answers were to be found somewhere in the Las Vegas area. Almost every one of the strange attacks was connected to the gambling mecca. The connection explained how people from other areas and even other countries could become a part of these mysterious occurrences. He was determined to make some sense out of it all.

A large billboard welcomed him to Nevada. What he saw out the windshield, however, only served to becloud his mood. The view reminded him of a painting he'd seen in an art museum years ago. The painting depicted another gloomy highway cutting through a similar landscape, sparse and lonely, apparently heading into infinity. As in the picture, the gradual darkness obliterated the scene until the earth and sky blended into a single shade of grey. He forced the image out of his mind and leaned forward, switching on the headlights.

In the distance, he noticed a car on the road's right shoulder. He continued to regard the car. As he drew closer, he could see someone in the process of changing the left rear wheel by the light of a small electronic lantern. He decelerated. When his headlights included the man in their illumination, the man gestured to him to stop. Draper could easily imagine himself in the same situation, so he pulled up behind the motorist. Leaving the engine running and the lights on, he exited to a cheerful greeting from the man, who stood next to his jacked-up car, lug wrench hanging from his left hand.

"Hey, thanks a lot for stopping. I was gittin' plumb tuckered out on this damned thing," the thin craggy face said in a Texas drawl. "Could you give me a hand?"

Walking toward him, Draper could see that he was quite old, maybe in his eighties, and clad in old cowboy boots, faced bib overalls, and a green flannel shirt. "Sure thing," he replied. "Too tight for you?"

"Yeah. I guess I just ain't as young as I used to be. A car ain't passed by here in the last half hour, so I figured I better give it a try myself. No luck, though." He stretched out his hand to the doctor, adding, "My name's Charlie Norman. I really appreciate your help."

"No problem. I'm Greg Draper."

The old man's weak handshake didn't belie his appearance. Norman explained that he was on his way to Las Vegas from outside of Santa Barbara, where he raised poultry. "I just have to get away from that chickenshit smell once in a while," he said, chuckling. "I get to thinkin' it gets into your damned pores if you don't take off every so often."

Draper grinned. "I'll bet that's not too far from the truth. Here, give me the wrench, and make some light here."

Kneeling to fit the tool onto the first lug nut, Draper did not sense the gas that rendered him unconscious.

Norman put the little canister on the ground next to him, then bent down to slip his arms under Draper's shoulders. Without apparent strain, he dragged him to the back door of his dusty old Pontiac and dumped him in the back seat. Norman went to Draper's car and shut it down, removing the keys from the ignition. He put them in his pocket and returned to his own car. He opened his trunk and reached inside for a small air pump. Setting it down near the left rear tire, he strung out its long cord into the front seat and stuck the plug attached to its end into the cigarette lighter socket, whereupon he returned to the pump. Picking up the valve at the end of a short red-and-black braided hose, he connected it to the stem of the flattened tire, switched on the machine and within two minutes inflated the tire.

He let the jack down, disconnected both ends of the pump, and returned the paraphernalia, including the gas canister, to the trunk of his car. Then he picked up the lantern and went to Draper's car, turned off its lights, and locked it. Finally, Charlie Norman got back into his own car, started it up, and drove eastward into the ever-darkening night.

CHAPTER 33

ollowing the other ship's ion trail, Troyer guided the
Vikinghaul with great care, settling on Titan's surface
eleven miles from the other's landing site. The security squad of nine men and three women, suited in orange and
fully armed, assembled outside. Shortly, Captain Troyer joined
them. He checked the intercom with the squad members and
began his briefing.

"Look," he said to them, "I don't know what we are going
to come up against, and I hope we don't have to use any force.
All I know for sure is that the other ship took off from Geneva
Station and ended up here. When we tried to hail them, there
was no answer. Just after they left, the station blew up. They
may have been responsible, or they may just be survivors. I
don't know how many people are on board, but I'm not taking
any chances. Their ship is a little over ten miles from here, so
we'll take the tracker. We're going to have to play it by ear, so
be careful, and don't get trigger-happy."

Troyer turned to see a six-wheeled vehicle that looked like a large panel truck emerge from the side of the *Vikinghaul,* He ordered everyone aboard. Climbing into the front cab, Troyer settled in next to Ezekiah Thaddington.

Thaddington, affectionately addressed by everyone as "Pappy" but never "Zeke," had been with Trent Enterprises more than half his life and often talked with great good humor of his escapades with Carl Trent in the early days of the company. In spite of continuing offers from Mr. Trent, he had never accepted a management position, maintaining that he was having too much fun and didn't want to be chained to a desk somewhere shuffling paper. The common believed was he drew more salary than anyone except Carl Trent himself, and Thaddington never tried to dispel the rumor. A rotund man over six feet tall and in his mid-sixties, he always seemed to have a three-day growth of white beard. He was the only Trent employee Troyer knew who, in the fitness-conscious company, sported what he himself proudly called his "grand-belly"—he weighed well over two hundred fifty pounds. He was invariably called upon to be Santa Claus at the Trent Christmas party, and, gentleman that he was, he happily performed the part. Troyer himself had known Thaddington for eight years and found him to be tough, reliable, and trustworthy.

They made their way quickly but carefully over the rough surface, the tracker's steel net wheels kicking up feathers of multicolored dust as Thaddington drove. Troyer sat watching the landscape, going over the possibilities in his mind. He realized the site would be dark when they reached their destination. They were heading in the same direction as Titan's rotation, and the terminator was already between them.

He turned to Thaddington. "If this isn't strictly a rescue mission, things could get very tricky, Pappy."

"Well, maybe, Captain, but you got a good group here. They won't get out of control—don't you worry."

"The scanners showed the ship in a valley, about a half mile ahead. We'd better hold up here. We'll go the rest of the way on foot."

When the tracker came to a stop, Troyer exited and assembled the squad outside. He told Thaddington to stay with the vehicle and stand by for his call. The rest checked their arms and equipment. After briefing them, Troyer led the group toward the hollow.

CHAPTER 34

Twenty three miles west of Las Vegas and almost an hour later, Charlie Norman turned right off the highway onto an unmarked, single-lane dirt road. He slowed down and drove carefully as the jerking wheel threatening to jump out of his wiry hands. His passenger shifted in response to the seat's movements, unaware of the jostling ride as the wheels tracked in and out of a multitude of ruts and potholes. The hazardous drive would have been difficult enough in the daylight but meant no small strain for the eighty-four-year-old man maneuvering it at night.

Three miles off the freeway, Norman stopped with the headlights directed toward a small, dilapidated building that looked like an oversized outhouse. He turned off the ignition but left the lights on and sat quietly for a moment, breathing evenly. As though resigned to his work, he inhaled deeply and sighed.

He exited the car, crossed in front of it, and wrestled his

unconscious passenger out of the back, half carrying and half dragging him to the front door of the worn clapboard structure. He reached up to the knob, unlatched the door, and pushed it wide open. The headlamps from the car revealed a dusty, windowless room devoid of furniture. Once more he struggled with Draper's form, pulling him over the threshold and laying him along the right side wall.

In the middle of the wood floor, the boards were supplanted by an incongruous eight-by-eight section of shiny metal. Searching through his pockets, Norman found a small metal box about the size of a cigarette lighter, one end of which he pointed in the direction of the silvery slab. After a push of his thumb on the top of the little box, the near edge of the polished rectangle jumped up an inch, then slowly began to rise. From below emerged a brilliant glare that transformed the inside of the rustic shack into a sallow blaze of almost blinding proportions. As the heavy cover stopped its travel at the vertical, the burnished underside, flawless as a sheet of glass, bounced the image of the two forms back, casting sharp shadows onto the bleak walls. Norman reached back with his foot and kicked the cabin door shut.

Wheezing with the effort, he picked up Draper by grabbing his arms and rolling him onto his own back in a fireman's carry, holding tightly onto the doctor's wrists. He paused for a moment, breathing heavily. In the middle of the space revealed by the opening in the trap door was a large white slab, precisely a meter wide and two meters long, upon which he arduously loaded the doctor, face up. Finished, he stepped back onto the wood floor, thumbed the little box again and watched as the platform lowered, carrying the unconscious man. When the platform descended below the level of the cabin floor, the great polished lid slowly closed. Once again the cabin was dark.

Norman stood in silence for nearly a minute, sweating profusely while his chest slowed its heaving. Then he sighed and opened the cabin's front door. Stepping out into the cool night air and the swath of the car's headlamps, he stopped, dug into his chest pocket, and extracted a pack of cigarettes, one of which he put to his crinkled lips. From another pocket, he took out a small round can and uncrewed the lid. Removing an old-style kitchen match, he struck it on the bottom of the cylinder and touched the flame to the end of his cigarette. He inhaled deeply, seeming to savor the smoke as it filled his lungs, then blew the blue-white cloud downward, observing the bright threads of smoke as they slowly dispersed in the quiet night air. The forgotten match flame began to burn his fingers. He quickly shook it out and threw it away.

He looked at the cigarette for a moment before dropping it into the dirt. He stepped on it, extinguishing it with a half turn of the sole of his boot, then continued around to the back of the car where he opened the trunk and reached inside. Barely able to distinguish anything in the dim red of the taillights, his boney right hand found and wrapped around the grip of an ancient forty-five caliber pistol that he had often shot at threatening sidewinders or coyotes. Once he had even used the gun to put one of his mares out of her misery after she broke her leg in a gopher hole. He always kept the gun loaded.

"What the hell," said Charlie Norman. Without hesitation, he swung the heavy old gun out of the trunk, pointed it at his own grizzled temple, and pulled the trigger.

Doctor Draper's journey on the slab began slowly, but its movement stirred him into foggy wakefulness. He opened his eyes to a seamless chrome ceiling sliding by above him. The ceiling curved to the right, and the slab followed, its speed increasing as the path sloped slightly downward to the point that he did not dare to jump off. After a few more seconds, the way straightened, and, with some effort, he rose up on his elbows to see what lay ahead.

The long tunnel seemed to have no end. Now, fully aware, he figured he was traveling at nearly fifty miles per hour. He gripped the sides as tightly as he could and felt the air buffeting his clothing while the combination of forces threatened to dislodge him. His stomach churned as he realized he would not be able to hold on much longer. He feared if he fell off, he could be caught up between the hurtling block and the walls of this accursed tunnel and torn apart and killed.

His ride began to decelerate. Draper could see what appeared to be a solid wall just a hundred feet ahead. He braced himself for the impact, but just a few yards short of what he'd thought was a dead end, the wall abruptly slid aside. He rode through without hesitation, after which the wall slipped tightly closed.

His ride slowed to a stop. He found himself inside a huge cave over a hundred feet long and he guessed about fifty wide.

The space was lit by a single horizontal line that ran along the wall completely around the room, about waist high. The center of the room was occupied by a large, silvery blob about the size of a small house. The blob seemed to be a semi-inflated balloon. Throughout the rest of the space were hundreds of empty tables. The space looked like an immense dining hall without chairs or place settings. Not twenty feet away from him, fifty naked men and women were clustered in a group, all watching him.

Feeling as though he had just been hustled into a nudist camp, Draper stood. "What the hell's going on here?"

CHAPTER 35

Alone in his office, Carl Trent sat at his desk sipping his second dry martini. He realized that his only grandson could very well be among those who, along with Mark Houston, were killed in the massive explosion at Geneva Station.

That huge project, which at first had been considered by even the imaginative as an impossible task, had taken years to finish. Its completion became the symbol of what a partnership of science and politics could accomplish. The entire world had followed the building process, many still disbelieving even as they watched on television. Only three lives had been lost in work accidents throughout the entire period from the first I-beam to the final rivet. A platinum plaque, located at the Communications Building front door, was dedicated to those who had perished. The christening and light-off of the nuclear power plants on the gigantic satellite were transmitted to a giddy world. Celebrations went on for the weekend in every part of the globe. The international companies that collaborated on the venture became financially secure. As a result of their success and the confidence of investors, worldwide prosperity seemed assured. Theorium, in fact, became a household word.

Carl Trent realized that the destruction of Geneva Station meant that transporting theorium from Saturn to Earth would probably be delayed ten to fifteen years. He also considered that this delay would change everything. The market price for theorium would be affected by the tremendous new costs involved in transportation, and there would be no new theorium—at least, not for some time to come. Its rarity now would be a factor in determining price, as with any commodity. This might be a good thing for some, he thought. There are always those who will take advantage of a situation. He snorted at the idea.

Then it occurred to him that Trent Enterprises would be in the catbird seat if for no other reason than his company had the most expert and practical knowledge of theorium, and that Trent Enterprises stood to gain the most from the present situation. Above all, Carl Trent was an astute businessman, As for the long run, he had no idea how the company might accomplish building another station like Geneva, but he knew the project would have to be given serious thought.

He brought his glass to his lips for a long pull. Then he stared at the almost-empty container in his hand. Carl Trent knew things were out of his control, and he was not used to that.

CHAPTER 36

Only thirty yards from the edge of the valley, Troyer waved the entire squad to the ground as the illumination ahead suddenly intensified. His first thought was that it was an explosion, and he fully expected a concussion wave to reach them while they were lying face down in the Titan dirt. After a few seconds, when nothing followed and the light did not diminish, he lifted his helmeted head, his heart pounding.

"Stay down," he said into the intercom. "Wait here, and be alert."

Thaddington's voice crackled in his earpiece. "Captain, it's Pappy. What's goin' on?"

"I don't know yet. Stay where you are till I get back to you. Troyer out."

With caution borne of military experience, he rose to all fours, constantly watching the rim of the canyon ahead. Seeing only the light, he continued to rise until he was in a high crouch.

He drew his hammer gun, setting it on maximum range. His heart resumed a slightly overworked throb as he walked toward the edge of the cliff that led to the plain below. Upon arriving, he spotted the source of the light a hundred yards distant where a pressure-suited figure, apparently armed, was urging two others ahead of him into a small block-like building. Before he could bring his binoculars to bear, they had disappeared inside.

Troyer radioed his crew to join him double-time. They followed as he slid with care down the treacherous slope. The cliff, apparently cut out of the red-orange sand, was completely devoid of rocks, so they could not maintain any kind of footing. Some continued to slide as best they could while others gave up the struggle to stay upright and simply tumbled down the long incline. Reconnoitering at the bottom, Troyer made sure no one was hurt, then readied them for an advance on the big ship and the structure that stood in the middle of the yellow glare.

With Troyer leading, they ran in zigzag pattern to the rear of the spacecraft that sat bathed in the blaze of the open pit. Finding no resistance, they slid themselves along the craft's outside skin to the entryway ramp. Troyer looked back at the ship's side: RETICULUM – Trent Enterprises.

"Sergeant Hawley," Troyer said, "take two inside and check it out." After the three left, the others settled themselves under the ramp.

Troyer studied the structure in front of them with its square opening about a foot deep and twenty feet wide. The floor itself was the source of the nearly blinding light. In the center was a seamless formation that seemed to be a large block of opaque brown glass with a doorway in the middle of the side facing them.

Several minutes later, his squad returned. They walked openly down the ramp, stopping when they saw Troyer. "The ship is empty, Captain," the sergeant reported. "No one at all is inside."

Troyer pointed to the structure just in front of them. "I saw somebody with a gun pushing some people inside that building. There's probably some kind of stairway or elevator inside. Anyway, we're going in after them. Set your guns to mid-range, and follow me."

As soon as the *Monitor* drew within sight of the *Vikinghaul*, Captain Ekstrom contacted First Officer Judy Nash and explained why he was there. He included a summary of the events surrounding the destruction of Geneva Station.

Nash reported that Troyer and his crew had disappeared into the canyon area, the site of the unidentified ship they had been following. She mentioned that Troyer's transmissions indicated possible trouble, that some of the people who had been manning the other ship were apparently being herded underground.

"I don't like this at all," she said. "There're only a dozen of us, and that damned ship is big enough to hold a couple hundred. If they're armed, as Captain Troyer seems to think, we could have some real problems here." His assistance, she told him, would certainly be welcomed, and she volunteered one of *Vikinghaul's* trackers.

"I appreciate that, Nash," Ekstrom said. "We'll be ready for the tracker in about ten minutes."

"Roger. It will be outside, sir. You need a driver?"

"No, thanks. I think we can handle it." He brought his small ship down within fifty yards of the great bulk of the *Vikinghaul*. As soon as the *Monitor* landed, Captain Ekstrom assembled his entire crew of sixteen to arm them before bringing them to the tracker proffered by First Officer Nash. A few minutes later they were loaded inside and ready to go.

"Oh, Captain Ekstrom?" Nash radioed.

"Yes?"

"Tracker One's driver is Ezekiah Thaddington."

"You mean Pappy?"

"Yes. You know him?"

"Sure I do."

"I guess everybody does." She smiled. "He's near the big hole on Bravo Three."

"Thanks, Nash. We'll be right back."

"Roger."

Ekstrom switched to the radio frequency Nash mentioned. "Tracker One—Pappy. This is Tracker Two—Pete Ekstrom. See anything interesting out there?"

"Well, Captain Ekstrom, good to hear your voice out here," a smiling voice returned. "No, all I got is one very juicy three-legged Titan lady who wants some company real bad. You want to give me a little assistance?"

"Yeah," he said, laughing. "On my way."

Ekstrom had driven smaller surface vehicles and was surprised and pleased with the directional stability and control the much bigger machine exhibited. On the way, Thaddington filled him in on what had taken place so far.

Once he arrived, instead of stopping well short of the gorge as Troyer had done, Ekstrom drove on nearly to the rim where he guided the vehicle along the edge, describing it to the more experienced Thaddington, asking about the probability that he could drive down the slope safely.

"The skipper said they went down on foot, but the stuff is like sand, so they ended up rolling most of the way," Pappy radioed back. "If there aren't any obstructions, you shouldn't have any trouble, though. I've made steeper grades than that. Just take it slow, and keep her pointed straight down as much as you can. Even if you do roll, just hold on—the weight distribution should land you on the wheels regardless." He gave Ekstrom the channels he could use to contact Troyer, adding, "Good luck, Captain. If you need me, give me a yell."

CHAPTER 37

Eli directed Mark and Carole to the right, waving to a row of small benches along the wall. "Sit down."

They sat on the first bench. To Mark's surprise, Eli put the sidearm into his waistband and sat facing them, only a few feet away.

"Oh, I wouldn't," Eli said, as if reading his mind. "The guardians"—he indicated the circling globes—"protect me. If you make the slightest move toward me, they'll deal with you."

Mark considered the globes. "Guardians. Yeah, we saw some of them on Geneva Station. They used some kind of beam to burn the guts out of Doctor Bradley and Rico Martinez."

"Sorry to hear that, but the guardians must have been threatened," Eli said. "They really are defensive and won't harm anyone unless Immana orders it."

"So, where are these people you want us to meet?"

"This"—he indicated the mound in front of them—"is the main body of intelligence that has been directing things from the start of this little venture. I say 'she' because the voice is female—she calls herself Immana—and she has total control over the guardians. They protect both of us."

"What voice?" Carole asked.

"The one she uses to communicate with me—in here." Eli pointed to his own head. "Something like telepathy. You really screwed up, Mark. Your destroying the injector and a couple of the guardians on Geneva are what caused the deaths of all those people back on Earth."

"Back on Earth? What deaths? You keep talking in riddles. What do you want with us? What's your involvement in all this?" He stopped and turned to Carole. "Wait a minute! You want to know what this bastard did? He sold his ass to this thing! That's the only way two spacecraft could have completely vanished. Less than a dozen people in the whole human race know how to fix it so the autobuoys would transmit nothing but garble—*and he's one of them!*"

Mark spun around to look directly at Eli. He leaned toward him, his brow furled and his eyelids tightened as he vented his wrath. "I thought you were my friend, you traitorous son-of-a-bitch. It's not only us. It's your father, the company, and who the hell knows how many others. Just how much are you getting paid? And what's happening on Geneva?"

Eli slid a few inches backward, sitting tall. He expression remained the same. "Immana has the ships and their car, Mark."

"Immana has them? Why the hell does she want them?"

171

"For a couple hundred years, they've been fighting with another race of—what can I call them—aliens, I guess. They need theorium for their weapons systems, and Geneva happens to be one of the few places in the universe that has the stuff. They could have procured the theorium in other ways, but they wanted to keep their presence a secret. That's why they used select human beings."

"That thing is in the middle of a war?"

"Immana is like a scout. I just happened to be one of the first people she contacted, and I was the only one smart enough to realize that If I didn't help them, their war would be brought into our galaxy. Now that they have what they need, they're going to leave. No one would have known they were here it you hadn't screwed it up."

"What the hell are you talking about?"

"You should have stayed out of it, Mark. When that machine was destroyed back there, you threatened Immana. To protect herself, she sent out messages to every person on Earth who has already been treated. The little chunk of her body in each of them connects them all telepathically. They're the ones who were going to be used to continue the project, in one way or another, but now they're not needed.

"As for Geneva Station, it doesn't exist anymore. It blew up shortly after we left. The reactors were set to overload." A scrofulous smile crossed his lips. "Something that big must have made one helluva spectacular fireball."

CHAPTER 38

The naked people in the room began to move toward Draper. For an instant, their advance brought fear of assault, but from their expressions, he realized they were simply curious. As the group gathered closer, one of the men nearest him spoke in a tentative voice. "Who are you?"

"My name's Gregory Draper. I'm a doctor. I was driving toward Vegas and—"

"—an old man who was trying to fix a flat stopped you, right?"

The voice that finished his sentence for him belonged to a young woman who pushed her way to the front of the crowd. She was pretty and well-formed with dark skin and the high cheekbones of an American Indian. He guessed she was about thirty, and from the deference accorded her by the others, she seemed to be the *de facto* leader of the group.

"Yes, and while I had my back to him, he must have knocked me out. The next thing I knew, I was on this crazy

173

ride on this table—or whatever it is. But how did *you* know that? What's your name?"

"I'm Commander Darla Sanders, Doctor, formerly skipper of the *Futura* from the Alkind Company's cargo fleet."

Alkind, Draper knew, was the theorium transport franchisee just prior to Trent. Some of their ships had been hired to help in the current operation.

"The way you got here," she continued, "is more or less the same way we all got here. The thing is, there's no way out."

"What happened to your clothes?"

"I don't know. I guess the old man took them as he went along, It's a pretty neat trick; sort of cuts down on the incentive to resist, doesn't it? How did you keep yours?"

"No idea, Commander Sanders, but you do make me wonder why. I woke up on the way here." He could see the place had no other doors and had apparently been cut out of the ground with no regard for ventilation. The prospect worried him since it suggested their captors didn't care whether they survived or not.

He pointed to the middle of the room. "What's that?"

"Some kind of machine," one of the men said, "but it acts like it's alive."

Draper advanced toward the affair in the middle of the room. His curiosity was most aroused by what appeared to be fifteen or twenty feet of large cable the thickness of a fire hose, inert on the side of the thing and coiled on the floor. He picked up the three-part end. Upon close examination, he saw that one segment contained a needle nearly a foot long with some sort of sac just before the point of attachment. He surmised that the sac probably held a sedative of some sort that it injected into the victim. The second part was composed of what appeared to be a suction cup.

When he picked up the third section, two small bits of brown material dropped to the floor from the tubelike open end. Even before he reached down to pick them up, he recognized them as identical in every respect to the small masses found in the skulls of Pollie Houston, Reginald Hawthorne, and all the others. Cold and heavy, the brown material felt like a small balloon full of mercury.

"Well, I'll be damned," he said. "Finally I know where they came from."

"What are you talking about?" the commander asked.

"Believe me, it's a long story. Were any of you implanted with these things?"

"What do you mean "implanted'?"

"That's what this contraption was doing," Draper explained. "Putting things into people's heads. Did anybody in the group seem to go crazy all of a sudden?"

"Yeah, I guess you could say that. Two people—a man and a woman. They attacked each other for no apparent reason. Their bodies are on the other side of the room." Sanders hesitated. "The woman choked the man with her bare hands so ferociously that she almost tore the guy's head off. Then she tried to eat his hand. She stuck his fingers in her mouth an—"

"Never mind, Commander. I know. I've been investigating this case for the last couple of days, and believe it or not, that type of behavior in not unusual. Was anyone else close to her when she died?"

"God, I don't know. We were all shocked." She asked the group if anyone had been near the two during the fighting. One young man worked his way forward.

"I saw the woman stop chewing on the man's hand, get up, and run directly at the wall not three feet from where I was standing. When she hit, she fell backward onto the floor. I went over to see if there was anything I could do, but her skull was cracked open. Blood was pouring out her ears and nose, and she was gurgling and spastic. Her eyes were wide open, rolled back."

Doctor Draper leaned forward, intent on the fellow's description. "What happened then?"

"She took a deep breath, looked squarely at me, and died."

"You saw something happen to her eyes, didn't you?" Draper insisted.

"Hell," the young man said, "you're going to think I'm nuts. I mean, I saw the color of her eyes change from blue to brown. It happened probably two or three seconds before she died."

Sanders, standing beside Draper, touched his arm. Her expression was puzzled. "You mind telling me what this is all about?"

He began explaining, but his exuberance evaporated almost as quickly as it had come. As he thought more, he realized the only way to tell if anyone had been injected with this insidious bit of stuff was to bring them to the point of death. The one other thing he could conclude was that this mass somehow made them go berserk. This information, as important as he'd thought, was useless as a practical matter.

"I thought I had the answer," he continued, "but what I found out doesn't really help. You can't go around killing people to find out if they're carrying this little monstrosity. This activity has been going on for a long time, yet only now are people going insane. Why?"

"I really don't care about that right now. We have to find some way to get out of here. Whoever trapped us in here must have figured we wouldn't be needing any food."

"There aren't any doors or windows in here?"

"None."

"What about the one I just came through?"

"We were looking for other exits," Sanders said. "I'm sure they—"

She paused as Doctor Draper approached the entry. As he reached out to touch it, the door began to slide open. He backed his hand away, and it reversed. Before it closed completely, he extended his hand back into the opening, whereupon it instantly reopened. Smiling, he turned to Sanders who rolled her eyes and shrugged.

"I think you're right," he said. "They didn't expect anyone would try to leave."

Naked thought they were, Commander Sanders and the others followed Doctor Draper back to the long shaft through which he had arrived. Some talked in twos and threes, others simply walked in silence. As he led them, Draper smiled considering how strange this must seem: he, the only clothed person, being followed like a pied piper by these thirty men and twenty women.

Well, at least we're getting out of this alive, which is something I wouldn't have been sure of just a short while ago.

When they reached the mouth of the tunnel, Draper realized they would have a few more difficulties. The cover of the hole was closed. There didn't seem to be any way for them to get out. The big metal doors were low enough that he could easily reach up and touch them. Strips in the floor, apparently some sort of magnetic tracks for the delivery system, ended there.

"We're safe for now," he told them, trying to make his presentation as reassuring as he could. "It's colder than the devil out there at night, so we may as well all get some rest. We'll figure something out in the morn—"

"Just a second, Doctor," Sanders broke in, stepping past him. She stretched her arm toward the shiny surface and smiled as some hidden machinery whirred. With a swoosh, the door lifted, and the cool night desert air began to spill into the tunnel. As she withdrew her hand, the door closed. Still grinning, she turned to Draper. "Well, I figured it might work just like the one back there." She flipped a thumb over her shoulder in the direction from which they had come.

"Very good, Miss Sanders," he said with mock sarcasm. "Well, I guess it's better we stay inside anyway—for now. Then I'll see if I can find some way to get clothing and something to eat for everybody. As I said before, I recommend we get some sleep and play the rest by ear. Sound good to you?"

"I suppose so. We don't have much choice, do we? At least it's warm enough in here." Commander Sanders went to the far corner of the space and sat facing into the angle. When she had made herself as comfortable as she could, she folded her arms on her knees and dropped her head onto them. The others milled about for a time, then found places to sit or lie. Mumblings of half-hearted goodnights were heard here and there. Moments later, most had nodded off. Draper noted with a smile that the men all grouped together, separate from the women. He wondered if they would have done so had they been fully clothed.

Draper found it difficult to sleep. He lay down along one wall, staring at the shiny surface above him, his hands clasped behind his head. He wanted to get out of this place now, but he knew that if he did, he had only a vague idea where he was, and he'd certainly get lost in the desert nighttime. He felt, like a stone in his stomach, a sense of urgency to let the world know what he knew, to somehow stop this incredible scourge.

Finally, seeing no alternative, he willed the tension to drain from him and closed his eyes.

CHAPTER 39

Wait a second." Mark glared at Eli. "You blew up Geneva Station?"

"Oh, no, I didn't do that. *You* did, and you're responsible for all their lives."

"You're out of your mind, Eli. I saw what that thing was doing. A couple hundred people were laid out on the tables. They were alive—I could see them breathing. What you're telling me is that machine was putting pieces of that alien into thousands of human beings so they could help get theorium for it?"

"You've got it pretty close, Mark," Eli said, smiling. "Immana has controlled the whole operation and everybody involved from the day it started. She created this implant that would give her total control of the people she needed. That's what you saw being done. That machine injects the thing right into the brain through the eye socket. I tell you, that son-of-a-bitch is a real marvel. The thing can't be detected because it absorbs all types of radiation. Not only that, but the entire group of implants acts as one. Whatever one learns, they all know. Immana controls individuals or the entire group.

"Our uses for theorium were allowed so the operation could continue undetected. There have been a few successful deliveries, you know. The stuff is vital to them, though."

"And where are the two shiploads of theorium and their crews?"

"Remember what happened to the *Sentinel*?"

Carole stirred. "Some kind of laser cannon that damned near killed us all. You destroyed the two haulers?"

"No, but the same method was used to disable them," Eli said. "The cargo is staked here on Titan. It's going to be picked up by another of Immana's ships."

"What about the crews?"

"They were getting their injections back there on Geneva. Mark's interference killed them all."

A ball of heat suddenly developed in Mark's stomach as anger surged through his body, but he grabbed the edge of the stone bench and willed it down. Eli's continual accusations about his killing people were grating on him. He calmed himself and said, "I still want to know what you're getting out of it."

"If I hadn't helped them, they would have taken the theorium anyway—only they'd have done it their way, without regard to consequences. At least, I kept it down to a few people who would have been returned after Immana was through. You screwed that up royally, and that's why they're dead."

Mark realized Eli was proud of his role in all this, and that he must be getting something out of it—something that would allow him to place no value on human life. He decided to keep him talking. "Why did they wait all this time?"

"They didn't want to alarm us, so they devised the implants. This wasn't the first approach they tried. The others just didn't work; the people couldn't be returned. People die every day and are never missed.

"If they don't get the theorium, their war will be brought to our system because this is the only place they can find it. If that happens, most of us will die anyway. With my help, they can get what they need and leave us alone."

"You wanted to know what I'm getting out of this. Saturn is my reward. You know what that planet is, Mark?"

"Sure," Mark said, puzzled, "it's basically a big gas bag."

"Saturn," Eli said with the air of a science teacher lecturing his ignorant students, "is a wonderfully complex planet with a solid core over four thousand miles in diameter. The robots who do the mining have to settle down through thirty thousand miles of gas before they get to the surface, and it's pretty cold down there."

"Yeah," Mark said, "something like three hundred degrees below zero. So?"

"Digging up theorium is only scraping the surface, old buddy. But below that, there's a lot more."

"Like what?" Carole asked.

Eli smiled again. "I'm going to be the richest man who ever drew a breath. And you two can become rich yourselves if you join me."

"Join you?" Carole scoffed. "Are you nuts?"

Mark waved his hand at her. "Hold on, Carole." The primary concern of the security officer in Mark was that he and Carole get out of this alive, but he also realized the only way he was going to get the whole story was to allow Eli to believe that his offer to them was being considered.

"Go on, Eli," Mark said.

Eli began to laugh—the distressing kind of chortle you receive when you're the butt of an elaborate practical joke. Eli paused, and his expression turned serious. "I'm going to drill. You know, for oil. It'll be the biggest challenge in human history. Below the topsoil, maybe a few hundred feet deeper than where the robots are digging now, Saturn is comprised almost totally of the purest carbon. Nothing else because that's all Saturn is: hydrogen, carbon, and methane. Under all that cold, swirling, unhealthy atmosphere where no human being can exist and only the toughest machines can work, is the largest, purest, most valuable diamond in the universe."

For the first time, Mark realized how perilous his and Carole's situation was. Eli wanted them to believe that what he was doing was helping the underdog aliens and at the same time saving humanity. The diamonds of Saturn were of no real consequence—Eli Trent, after all, was already extremely wealthy. Mark knew one thing that was more attractive than money or even diamonds, and Trent's grandson had now had a taste of it. Eli had become familiar with the heady feeling of control—of power. Carl Trent never surrendered but the smallest share of his own power to his grandson. Eli now had his own, which he had already used to devastating effect.

Mark was certain of something else, too. Eli would not have told them all he had unless he intended to make the offer to join him an ultimatum. If they refused, as of course they would, Eli would have to kill them both. The foreboding fell upon him like a great ray cloud, prodding his defenses, launching his mind to race.

A slight hissing interrupted their conversation. Their heads turned in the direction of the sound. A small but rapidly spreading hole, accompanied by hot metal spattering and vaporizing, appeared in the exact center of the set of doors through which they had come earlier.

Alerted, the guardians converged and moved toward the area. They formed a line just in front of Immana as if they were drones protecting a queen bee.

Mark took advantage of the distraction. While Eli's head turned toward the noise and commotion, Mark delivered a backhand slap-punch to his right temple from a tightly closed fist. Eli grunted and fell unconscious to the floor. Mark grabbed the hammer gun and, with Carole crouching beside him, began firing at the guardians.

Several of the globes broke away from the others, swooping toward them like dive bombers. Mark's shots were unerring. The first two globes disintegrated before they could get close. Immana, however, had apparently learned something from the experience on Geneva: the little weapons did not follow one another as they had before. Three broke away and circled the chamber, seeming to want to pick their own time to attack. The others remained within a few feet of Immana's peak.

The hole in the doors had expanded to a circle several feet across. The business ends of at least a half dozen lasers and hammer guns poked their way in. The guardians streaked around the room searching for targets. As the opening in the door continue to enlarge, two of Troyer's uniformed crew stepped through, their weapons at the ready. One guardian looped down and accelerated along the wall toward the pair, unnoticed by either of th—

Carole screamed and pointed. Even as they turned to look, the sphere swept between them. The men did not see it until it was too late. Spitting out its ugly death, the sphere crumpled both men amid agonizing screaming and clawing at spreading wounds. A third member of the rescue team, climbing through the hole, shot the globe out of the air. Other team members made their way into the room, firing in every direction, lighting the chamber like an electrical storm.

"Get to the airlock and pick up our helmets!" Mark yelled to Carole. He had begun to smell the outside atmosphere and realized they were in danger of suffocating. "Bring all three. I'm taking this bastard with us!" Carole hurried toward the opening.

Mark grabbed Eli's collar. His shoulder painfully reminded him of its condition as he pulled the unconscious form, occasionally firing at guardians. He gritted his teeth and let his anger override the irksome pain.

Reaching through the burned-out hole in the doors, Carole picked up their helmets and spun around. Mark was a few feet behind her, grimacing with the pain and effort. She handed him two helmets. He slipped one over Eli's head and the other over his own. Carole donned hers, took a welcome deep breath, and reached back to assist Mark. Together they dumped Eli into the airlock where he remained, sprawled.

"Stay here," he told her, and darted back through the hole, weapon in hand.

Amid the tumult were Mack Troyer, Pete Ekstrom, and their crews blasting away in every direction as the guardians swooped and streaked and were destroyed. Mark had only one target in mind. He contrived to position himself so he could get a clear shot. Walking with acute deliberation, he squeezed off a direct hit on one of the last guardians as it headed toward him. He stopped twenty yards from the huge bulk in the middle the room and trained his weapon on it.

The pandemonium subsided as the others stopped to watch him, all the guardians having been destroyed. Somehow, everyone realized the battle was not over.

In front of Mark, the mass underwent a change. Its upper surface, already almost touching the ceiling, swelled even higher. It quivered and became a deeper, darker brown, almost black. Slowly, from within, a sound issued forth, rising in pitch and volume. At first, the sound was only a vibration, something Mark felt rather than heard. The tremor seemed to craw on his skin like the first chill on a cold, wet night. The tone became shrill as the frequency increased and took on properties that made it almost a human scream, growing louder and louder. The shriek sunk into his brain, threatening to disorient him.

He felt a searing in his eyes and blinked—two, three times —to soothe them, to stop the burning sensation. He thought he must have somehow gotten smoke or some debris in them. They started to produce tears with the liquid accumulating so quickly that his vision blurred. He wiped them with his left hand, but there was no stopping it. The pistol in his extended right hand became heavy, and another pain began in his right elbow.

A whistle went off inside Mark's head, and he could not hear. His heart pounded in his chest. *This damned thing is trying to kill us with noise.* With a wrenching mental effort, Mark fought through the torture and put both hands on the hammer gun. Willing himself to a single purpose, he brought the gun to bear directly on the middle of the great dark bulk in front of him.

This warrior is Immana. Immana is part of the conflict in which she is the last hope of her kind. She was sent to bring back what her comrades need to continue their fight. If she fails, they face oblivion. The victors can continue to spread their horrors among the stars, and, if it happens the way Eli says it will, they might eventually find their way here, to our own system. The result could be the annihilation of all mankind.

Sorry, Immana. You can't do it that way.

Mark squeezed the trigger. The single yellow beam entered the undulating blob of quicksilver and was absorbed into it.

Nothing happened.

Something must be wrong. In the pit of his stomach, he felt a seed of fear that he had made a terrible mistake.

Immana bulged and squirmed. She seemed to be trying to detach herself from the floor, to defy gravity in her attempt to flee from this terrible beam that had entered her, and she screamed. Inside all their minds, long and lamentingly, she wailed, as though she had become aware that to struggle was useless, that her goal was impossible, that she had lost. The ululation trailed off, and Immana collapsed and disintegrated into a mass of smoldering flesh only a few inches high.

CHAPTER 40

G o ahead," Troyer told Ekstrom as he touched his helmet's holocam start button. "I'm ready."

Captain Ekstrom pressed this detonator, and the group of aluminum-clad men and women watched from nearly a mile away as the *Reticulum* and the entire surface surrounding it for fifty yards first lifted almost ten feet, then fell back on itself. Red and white plumes of flame spewed through a string of fractures, followed by a tremendous blast which shook the ground beneath their feet. While clouds of dust filtered slowly back down through the atmosphere, Troyer turned to Ekstrom.

"That takes care of that," he said, handing him the tape. "As soon as you get clear, transmit a copy of that to the company. Tell them we'll give them the whole story when we get back." He nodded toward Eli Trent, who stood quietly in handcuffs. "Take this guy and keep him locked up.

Thaddington will go with you. And have the company send help. I know a couple of other cargo vessels are close by. Have them arm their crews. We're going for the missing theorium, and we may have some more problems. Besides, my ship won't be big enough if we do recover the stuff."

"Okay, Mack. My security people will stay with you. Pappy and I will make sure Trent gets back. Good luck."

"Thanks, Pete. Now let's get the hell out of here."

Ekstrom, Thaddington, and Trent marched off toward the *Monitor.* Mark, pausing at the big ship's entry door, turned to watch the three getting into the smaller vessel. He shook his head, saddened and angry.

Aboard the *Monitor,* Ekstrom went forward and pulled himself into the pilot's seat while Thaddington took their captive to one of the sleep pods where he set its controls to keep Trent in suspension until they arrive on Earth. That done, he rejoined the captain.

Applying full power to the lifting engines, Ekstrom urged the vessel to rise above the surface of Titan. Once it had lifted to five hundred feet, the vessel veered off and accelerated out of sight to begin its three-week trip back to San Diego.

Captain Troyer, using the information obtained from a reluctant Eli Trent, headed the *Vikinghaul* in the opposite direction, in search of the *Baronhaul* and *Princesshaul.* Trent told them that Immana had made him aware that others of her kind would be coming within a few hours to retrieve the theorium on board the two ships that were now resting in a large depression on the other side of Titan. "If these others are unable to get the theorium," Eli had said, "the war already going on against Immana and her race will certainly spread into our solar system."

Mark and Carole sat enjoying dinner in the captain's cabin. Mark was being tended to by one of the ship's medical staff, a young woman, who carefully cleaned and bandaged his shoulder wound as he ate. Troyer reclined in a chair behind his desk.

"What puzzles me," Carole said, "is that these creatures apparently need others to do their work." She used her fork to emphasize her point. "They seem to have some kind of mental process that controls people, but without outside agents, they aren't any more than a pile of flesh. They don't have arms or legs or hands. How did they even get here? They had to have a ship of some kind, but even if they did, how did they control it? With their minds?"

"Maybe they did, Carole," Mark said. "You saw what they could with those damned globes. Maye they literally have the power of mind over matter."

"If they do," Troyer said, "why would they use human beings and spacecraft to get theorium off the surface of Saturn? Why didn't they just levitate the stuff up?"

"I don't know, Captain," he said. "Maybe there are limits to what they can do. Or maybe they just like the idea of having slaves."

"Well, whatever it's all about, they're damned sure not going to import their war here if I have anything to say about it," Troyer said.

"Seems to me," Carole said, "they already have."

Messages trickling in from the *Vikinghaul* were relayed to Carl Trent's office by Ed Masterson. His delivery was as matter-of-fact as he could make it.

"First Officer Nash says Troyer followed the other ship to Titan. Upon landing, they saw hostages being taken below the surface and went in after them. The *Monitor* arrived and Ekstrom and his crew followed Troyer inside. Some fighting followed and a few casualties resulted, all among Ekstrom's crew. The hostages were Captain Banning and Mark Houston. According to this, the bad guy was Eli."

"What!" Trent's eyes narrowed. "What are you talking about?"

"They're still debriefing Banning and Houston as we speak. Ekstrom is on his way back here in the *Monitor* with your grandson. No other names were sent, so we don't know what's happening with Banning's crew. I expect we'll be getting more on that later."

"Just a second here. My grandson is in custody?"

"Yes, sir. The latest message went into some detail on the destruction of Geneva Station. According to Nash, your grandson, Banning, and Houston were on the vessel that left just before the station went up. They knew there were hundreds of people still there when Geneva exploded." He hesitated, knowing what he was about to tell Trent was going to be difficult for him to believe.

"Well?"

Masterson shifted his eyes to the papers in his hand, then back to Trent, feeling as though he was about to betray a friend. "Banning and Houston said the *Reticulum*, the ship they left Geneva on, was being run be Eli, and, from what they said, he was the one who blew up the station."

Carl Trent came out from behind his desk in a huff, his eyes fiery and his brow wrinkled. "What the hell are you talking about! My grandson responsible for killing hundreds of people and destroying Geneva Station? Bullshit, Masterson! He would never do anything like that. It doesn't make any sense."

Masterson backed up a step, his eyes wide. "Mr. Trent, all I'm doing is relaying the information."

"Listen. You figure it out," Trent angrily shot at him. "The *Reticulum* is one of the old cargo vessels. No one person can run one of those big bastards by himself; it takes a crew of twenty! How the hell can one person lift off in an old cargo vessel, race all over the sky, and then land on Titan—all alone? If Houston and Banning were with him, they had to be helping him."

"Mark Houston doesn't know anything about running a cargo vessel," Masterson said. "Banning does, but—"

He realized continuing this line of talk was tantamount to agreeing that Eli Trent was to blame, and he was addressing the man's grandfather. He switched gears. "They've asked for some backup and another cargo vessel, so I've dispatched the *Mastiff* and *Stellarhaul*—the other two ships in the sector—to Titan. They were close by, so both should be there shortly. Also, I'll be talking with Troyer myself, sir. I want to find out what they were able to discover about the two missing ships and what happened to the *Sentinel.* I don't feel like waiting a month until they get back here."

"Go ahead. Let me know what you find out. And I want the full story on Eli. I don't like what you're telling me."

"Absolutely," Masterson said, letting himself out. He was glad to be done with that conversation.

CHAPTER 41

With every relevant piece of equipment on board put to work seeking the position of the two stolen ships, the huge mass of the *Vikinghaul* slowly trekked over the crazy-quilt surface of Titan at ten thousand feet, making great swings east and west as it progressed north toward the small planet's pole. Everyone watched the bridge computer screens as the three-dimensional images crept by in response to the ship's course and speed, searching for the first signs of the area described by Eli Trent. A planet over three thousand miles in diameter had a lot of large depressions, and Troyer was beginning to think that Trent was as much a liar as he was demented.

Mark's vigil at the moment was also only partial. He was trying to piece his personal life together and finding it difficult. He knew now that he never loved Pollie, and that he had succumbed to her seduction mostly because he had lost Carole —or thought he had. Sex, at the time, was the driving force in his life; Pollie exemplified everything thunderingly sexual to him, and he had been thinking with his genitals. But Eli, deranged as he might be, had been right about his marriage.

The time had come to decide. That Pollie was lying in a hospital didn't matter. *Am I supposed to continue with this mistake just because she's injured? Am I supposed to wait until she's well to lay the bomb on her? The outcome is inevitable, so why delay?* On top of everything else, she was the one who had made the move when she walked out the door with Jerry Lucas.

And now there was Carole: the right place, the right person, the right time. He glanced over to her position across the expanse of green carpet that covered the floor of the flight control area. Somewhere she had found a black, form-fitting uniform—a leotard-like slip-on—cinched with a three-inch wide white leather belt and finished off with a pair of white half-calf boots. *One thing they have in common; they both know to dress.* With desire and fascination Mark watched the supple muscles of her back and shoulders as she moved to touch the keypad in front of her.

No, he thought, *too much water is over the dam.* In six years, Pollie never worked at their relationship. From the beginning, she'd made a pretense of caring, and Mark had bought it. Their relationship was simply a convenience, he saw now, a way for Pollie to have the opportunities to which the Trent association led and to be part of the social group. None of the things one might expect from a marriage were forthcoming. There was lovemaking, but no love—not even friendship. He knew their interaction was phony from the first day, but it boiled down to his refusing to admit to having made such a gross mistake. They pretended a lot in those six years, and the day she left crowned it all.

Carole. She was genuine, warm and passionate, and she worked at their interaction. She made him feel that he needed her in his life, although he didn't realize that until she came back into it. Mark was happy when she was with him, even through the chaos of the last few days. He smiled, remembering her refusing his shirt back on Geneva. There was a little bit of perversity in that gesture, and he knew that she knew it. *I'm going to tell Pollie as soon as we get back, and we can take the final step and end this marriage. Hell, it won't be a surprise to her.* He was determined that this second opportunity would not be wasted.

"There they are," Captain Troyer announced, interrupting Mark's thoughts. The display showed a deep rent in the surface a mile from their present position, a few hundred miles from the Titan north polar area. The rent measured three hundred yards long and eighty wide, inside of which were nestled two large cylinders that the computer identified as the missing ships. They saw no signs of life and no indication of an entry or cavern such as had been at the previous site.

Communications informed Troyer that Captains Lisa Ingersoll of the *Stellarhaul* and Gordon Hastings of the *Mastiff* had radioed, calling to assist. He was told they were a little more than an hour away.

"Let them know where we are, and have them set Alert One," he said. "Tell them to meet with me here as soon as they get down. This time, I want nobody hurt. I don't give a damn what the sensors say about no life being around. We take no chances. We're going in ready for anything, and we're going in from above."

The *Vikinghaul* descended, twelve landing jets squirting out blue-white flames to counter Titan's weak gravitational pull. Dust clouds billowed out from the craggy underside of the ship as eight cushioning struts touched their shock-absorbing pads to the surface.

CHAPTER 42

For Draper to remember where he was took a moment. The gleaming metal bid him a cheerless morning, and he turned his head to see the others, some of whom were already stirring. 7:35 a.m. He groaned, slowly moving his arms and legs to stimulate circulation and encourage some looseness of limb. His shoulder muscles protested, and he felt aches in nearly every joint of his body. "I'm too old to be sleeping on a bare floor," he said to no one in particular.

"Where's my bacon and eggs?" It was Sanders.

"The kitchen isn't open yet," someone answered. "The cook is late." Light laughter rippled around the space. Everyone seemed to be awake. Draper was glad the group had maintained some semblance of humor. He supposed that the inevitability of the situation had a little to do with this, in addition to no one's having any physical secrets—they wore no clothes—both of which tended to make people look outside themselves. Whatever it was, the group's humor was comforting to him.

Draper got to his feet and stretched. "I'm going to take a look around. I'll be right back." He reached his hand over his head, and the silvery slab promptly responded, swinging up to allow in a swath of cool air. Though it was daytime, the colder air had been trapped inside the cabin, and it dropped a chilly wave onto the group's bare skin.

"Hey, who opened the fridge?" someone yelled.

Three men came to help as Draper pulled himself up into the room above. He stood in the interior of the small cabin with its front door open, swing in against the wall. The only sounds were a chipping and a low rustling like pieces of leather rubbing together in the wind. After a moment, he cautiously stepped toward the doorway, keen for anything that might indicate someone's presence. He reached out to rest his hand on the doorframe and inched further until he could see outside.

A few small scrubs were visible in an otherwise flat, barren stretch of open desert. The building from which he looked out seemed to be the only man-made object in view except for an undistinguished, dusty, thirty-year-old Pontiac, in front of which lay the body of a man. A dozen or so vultures were dancing and jumping around the corpse, flapping their wings, tearing and nipping at the body. One was halfway into the stomach cavity, frantically pulling at something inside, while another rammed its beak into what remained of the top of the man's head, tugging at and swallowing some chink of bloody flesh. Even at this early morning hour, the sun was quickly bringing its warmth onto the scene, and thousands of flies were buzzing, dipping, and whirring as they tried to scavenge their own small share of the corpse. The car's headlights burned a lazy yellow in the morning light.

Draper stepped out of the cabin and approached the body, waving his hand to shoo the scurrying birds away. They moved off a few feet but eyed him without fear as he bent over what he recognized as Charlie Norman's lifeless form.

"What the hell happened to you?" he asked aloud, a questioning frown on his face. Methodically, he began going through the pockets of the old man's overalls, fanning the flies away as he proceeded. In one pocket he found two sets of keys, which he retrieved. One he recognized as his own. The other he guessed contained the ignition key to the old car that sat behind them.

"Sorry, old friend, but I'm going to need your car." He gave the keys a quick toss in the air as he went to the driver's side of the vehicle. "Let's hope there's still enough left in the battery." No longer threatened, the hungry flies and vultures returned to their grisly work.

Slipping into the front seat, Draper looked for the switch and turned the lights off. He picked out the ignition key among the dozen or so on Norman's ring and tried it in the slot, pleased that it fit. He turned it with a silent prayer that the car would start. The first turns of the starter were weak and sickly, and his heart sank, but just as it seemed the battery had spent its last gasp of energy, the engine roared to life. Draper breathed a sigh of relief and smiled as the birds fled, frightened by the noise. He added a blast of the horn, just to provide an exclamation point to them, and watched them take flight.

The old Pontiac had half a tank of gas, so he left the engine running and exited the car. As he walked back toward the cabin, he saw a pistol on the ground near the right front wheel.

What happened to Norman, and where did this revolver come from?

He stopped a foot away from the gun and considered picking it up, but rejected the idea and went into the cabin. Draper stomped on the hatch, and a few seconds later, it opened. Sanders stood with several of the others directly in the middle of the space, her hand extended, supporting the open hatch.

"Well, Doc, that was fast. What's up?"

"I found the old man's body outside. The buzzards got to it. His car is here, too, and it has almost a half tank of gas. I wanted to let you know that I'm going to take it and get help. It shouldn't be too long, so sit tight."

"Okay. We'll be all right."

"See you later."

"We'll be here." Sanders dropped her arm, and the cover closed.

Draper left the cabin and climbed back into the car. He put the car in gear and drove away, following the tracks it had made the night before.

CHAPTER 43

Captain Troyer called the meeting with Ingersoll and Hastings in his ready room on the *Vikinghaul.* The briefing was to the point. "When we get to the place where the ships are, we will determine whether or not the *Baronhaul* and the *Princesshaul* are damaged. If they are, we'll assess the extent of the damage, and, if necessary, we'll transfer the theorium from them to the *Vikinghaul*," Troyer said.

"The *Mastiff* will act as security. She's well-equipped with laser and plasma cannons, but I don't think we'll need anything like that. Our primary mission is to get the theorium back, so, if it looks like we're going to be here for a while, we'll make provisions for the theorium. Make sure everyone knows what they're supposed to do. Any questions?"

There were none, so Troyer dismissed them to their own ships.

Captain Ekstrom joined Mark, Carole, First Officer Nash,

and the rest of the flight officers on the bridge of the *Mastiff*. Standing in front of his master control position, he began to brief them on what he planned to do.

"I'm going to set this ship down as close as I can to the other ships. The *Stellarhaul* will set down next to us, and we'll join forces outside. The *Mastiff* will be holding a couple of thousand feet over us, just in case. We'll check to be sure, but preliminary indications are that the *Baronhaul* and *Princesshaul* are in such bad shape they won't be able to lift off. That means we'll have to transfer the theorium to this ship and the *Stellarhaul*, which will be a lot of work for all of us.

"If we do have a fight on our hands, certain people are not expendable. They will stay behind until the shooting is over. If necessary, they will take off and head home. They include: the first officers and navigators of all three ships; their skeleton crews; and Houston and Banning here." He looked at Carole and Mark. "You two have to get back at all costs, so I'm transferring you both to the *Mastiff*. Unless and until we need you out there for loading, you stay put. Is that understood?"

"I guess so," Banning said.

"How about you, Mr. Houston?"

"I understand. And thanks for getting us out of that mess back there."

"You're welcome. Now both of you move to the *Mastiff*." He turned to the others. "Okay, gang, let's get some work done."

Carole and Mark exchanged brief looks of resignation and left the bridge. Outside the door, Mark took her by the arm and swung her around to face him. Looking at her, he sensed a frustration that he, too, felt. They wanted to be in on whatever happened—directly.

"You know he's right, don't you?" Without waiting for her answer, Mark continued, " I'm sure that you'd like to be right in the thick of it, and so would I. We're not the kind of people who sit around and wait for things to happen, but in this case, we don't have a choi—"

"Mark"—she placed her index finger on his lips—"in this case, I don't mind that much." Her eyes seemed to sparkle as a quick smile danced over her mouth. Her arms slid around his neck, and she pulled his face to hers. She pouted her lips to kiss him, and when he did likewise, she playfully bit down on his lower lip, just hard enough to make him jump back in surprise. Laughing, she grabbed his hand and pulled him as a small child would a playmate. "Let's go," she said.

He exercised his strength and prevented her from any further movement. She turned, and seeing his eyes, stopped her resistance, allowing herself to be brought toward him.

He locked his gaze onto hers and clasped her hand to his chest, bending her arm and forcing her closer. Her eyes were like liquid amber, flashing as she looked first at one side of his face and then the other. She moved into his arms and again encircled his neck. He wrapped her in his arms, bringing their bodies into full contact. He felt his heart pounding, and then she smiled. Her warmth seemed to overwhelm him. He could not and would not stop now. He wanted her to know what he had to say, and though he groped for some new words, some way to create an indelible impression on her, he could think of but a solitary expression.

"Carole, I love you. I'm sorry that we've spent an eternity apart, but I promise it will not happen again."

"I love you, too, Mark."

"Well, I want you for the next eternity, and I'm going to make sure of it."

She said nothing further.

Mark felt a deep happiness, a sense of lightheadedness, for the second time in his life. Her body fit his he knew with a certainty he had never felt before, and the feeling was warm and secure and contented.

Mark took her uplifted face in his hands, gazing at her from only a few inches. He wondered how he could have made the mistake he had made so long ago and had no answer. *Finding an answer is not what needs to be done now.*

He held her and bent his head. His lips came closer to hers, her eyes closed now. He recovered in that moment, like a fish that has been returned to the water after being out of it for a long time. He felt reawakened, engulfed in joy.

Their kiss was long and fervent, a tiny incident that might have made little difference in the universe of so many important events, but to Mark, it was the fulfillment of the promise that caressed his heart.

For anything more to be said was unnecessary. They left the ship arm in arm, smiling at each other like two children who have just discovered something that only they share.

CHAPTER 44

The police arrived at the Draper home just before noon to talk to a worried Debbie Draper who had called them after she contacted the hospital and discovered they had not heard from her husband since the previous morning.

She had become more apprehensive when inquiries to other hospitals and among their friends revealed nothing, It was not like Greg to be gone for nearly twenty-four hours without some word, and with all that had been happening, she was concerned for his safety. To hear the news of the death of Doctor Hawthorne had frightened her even more, even though Kensington provided only the barest details. When she inquired as to how he died, she was asked to wait, whereupon a police lieutenant came on the line. After ascertaining her identity, he asked why she wanted to know the cause of death. She answered that he was a friend of theirs, and was told that he had apparently committed suicide, which seemed a little far-fetched. Something wasn't right about that. Her response to Greg when they had had the discussion about Hawthorne not investigating the cranial tumors and now the latter's sudden demise gave her a feeling of foreboding. Now she was beginning to think that all these events somehow tied together, including her husband's absence.

Nevertheless, in her conversation with the two officers, she deigned not to include that information. They, in fact, already knew who Gregory Draper was, and most of the discussion concerned such things as the condition of their marriage, who might wish to harm him, and other more or less routine queries. The officers were courteous and businesslike, but seemed more interested in the possibility that the doctor had been kidnapped than anything else. One of them asked if they had any enemies and wanted to know if the doctor had had any problems with any medical cases recently. She answered that there were no problems of which she was aware, and that seemed to satisfy the officers.

Whether or not Gregory Draper could be considered missing was in question because the period of time was too short. The usual time was more than forty-eight hours. Her anxiety notwithstanding, the situation just wasn't serious enough at this point, they said. Before they left, they gave her details on how to call them if she was contacted by anyone about her husband. They assured her that they would get the word to all the local authorities to keep an eye out for him and supplied her with a contact card. She thanked them as they left.

The house was quiet once again.

She went into the kitchen and opened the cabinet above the range, taking down a small expresso coffeemaker. From a canister on the counter, she removed the rich black grounds of Italian coffee with a teaspoon and packed them lightly into the machine's basket. She was about to complete preparations when her cell sounded.

"Hello."

"Hi. It's me, honey." Draper's voice came through the instrument with a smile.

"Oh, my God, Greg, where have you been? Are you all right?" Debbie spoke rapidly, unable to hide the concern and fear she had been going through over the last twenty-four hours. "The police just left—I called them when I didn't hear from you. I tried to reach you at the hospital—Doctor Hawthorne's dead. They said he committed suicide. Nobody knew where you were. What's going on?"

"I'm sorry, Debbie. I'm fine." His tone changed to apologetic seriousness. "I just couldn't get in touch until now. I'm in the desert, about a hundred miles west of Las Vegas. I was trapped underground last night."

Her expression turned incredulous. "What?"

"It's a long and crazy story, honey. And I know about Hawthorne. Just listen."

He related what had taken place from the time he left the office the evening before, leaving out only the grisly details of Hawthorne's demise. Even as he related the rest of the story, he realized how fantastic it must have sounded.

She continued making the coffee while he spoke: pouring in the water, plugging in the machine, and turning it on. By the time he brought her up-to-date, steam was hissing as the hot brew dripped into the glass pot. Debbie removed the coffee and slid it under the small chrome tube. With her other hand, she opened the jet so that the steam gurgled and swirled the mixture, filling the kitchen with the delectable, pungent aroma.

"What's that?" he interrupted himself to ask.

"I made some espresso," she said. "Want some?"

"Funny."

"All those people were naked?"

"What? Yeah."

"That must have been fun. This Commander Sanders. Is she good-looking?"

"I suppose so."

"You mean you didn't look?"

"Honey, I'm a doctor," he said, trying not to sound defensive.

"'Honey, I'm a doctor'," she mocked. "What does that mean? That you didn't look or you did look?"

"She's not nearly as pretty as you are. Sounds like a little green monster there."

"Just protecting my interests," she said.

He could tell she was smiling. "Good—for a second I thought you were going to tell me you were contacting a lawyer." He paused. "You're the first one I've called, Debbie. Now I've got to get these other people taken care of. I left them a couple of hours ago, and they're tired and hungry. As soon as I get that done, I'll be on my way home. Please don't worry anymore."

"I'll worry until you get here. I'll call the police and tell they you're okay . . . Greg?"

"What?"

"I love you."

"I love you, too, honey. See you soon."

CHAPTER 45

The *Stellarhaul*, the *Vikinghaul*, and the *Mastiff* lifted off the Titan surface at the same moment. The *Mastiff* climbed high, to four thousand feet, then leveled off. Captain Troyer, commanding all three, kept the *Stellarhaul* slightly ahead of Captain Ingersoll's maintaining both ships at two hundred feet. Synchronizing, they moved off toward the location of the *Baronhaul* and the *Princesshaul*.

From the vantage of the *Mastiff's* large front port, Mark and Carole watched their approach to the area from where they sat strapped into the right side pair of swivel observation seats mounted on either side of the bridge. Hastings sat in the captain's chair surrounded by its console squarely in the center of the bridge. Four hundred yards away, two large spacecraft could be seen resting, one in front of the other. Large black letters on their light green sides spelled out their names. Saturn's shadow created a terminator just beyond the site, creeping slowly toward them and spilling something like black lava into the far edge of the depression. The totality of the effect was surprising from their altitude. The little moon's colorful veneer disappeared behind the sharp edge of darkness with almost no transition.

"In a few minutes, it's going to be night down there," Mark said. "I wonder if Captain Troyer figured that in when he worked all this out."

Hastings, Ingersoll, and Troyer continued their dialogue, adjusting their ships' courses at speeds to coordinate their assignments. The *Stellarhaul* slowly passed over the near edge of the site, its looming shadow drawing to within fifty yards of the downed cargo ships. The *Vikinghaul* followed, and then both accelerated under Troyer's orders, swiftly skimming the ground toward their target.

Captain Ingersoll pulled her ship to a stop over the assigned spot and fired landing jets for the descent. Pods extended, the craft touched down and settled, its underside lights flooding the area in brilliant white. Almost immediate, both side hatches opened, ramps descended, and the crew swarmed onto the surface, arms at the ready. They assembled in silence in an illuminated circle just forward of the big cargo craft, waiting. A few looked up, having noticed the *Mastiff* floating above them.

Troyer watched the ominous blackness of the terminator as it approached their position, moving, it seemed to him, all too quickly. He wasted no time docking the *Vikinghaul* only a few yards from the *Stellarhaul,* adding his own outside lighting to the scene.

With Sergeant Hawley in charge, the teams from both ships

joined and began to move toward the two silent hulks. Troyer and Ingersoll monitored their progress, gazing at their holocreens. Hawley spoke to his troops, marshalling them into three squads of ten each. The first walked toward the area between the two ships, while the other two followed a few paces behind.

"Hastings," Troyer radioed, "how are you doing up there?"

"Reading you loud and clear, Captain. Everything's fine," he answered. His voice was flat. "It's quite a view from up here. I can see them moving in. Everything going okay down there?"

"Seems to be," came the reply. They were heading toward the front of the *Princesshaul,* about fifty feet away.

"Captain Troyer!" Hawley called.

A silvery teardrop shape, about the size of a large automobile, emerged from the *Princesshaul's* forward cargo doors. In an instant, the shape was flooded with white, the lights having been zeroed in by the sensors detecting its motion. The shape seemed to have a fluid surface. Moving with high speed and in silent ease, it came to a standstill midway between the *Baronhaul* and the *Princesshaul,* looking every bit like an oversized drop of mercury.

"I see it," Troyer said. He smiled to himself, seeing that Sergeant Hawley had already alerted his forces. *These guys know what the hell they're doing.* They had spread out and were lying on the ground, their weapons pointed at the strange, quivering mass glinting in the bright floodlights.

As they watched, a spinning motion appeared a quarter of the way from the top of the mass and directly in front of them, as if a small propeller were turning just under the thing's skin. The spinning seemed to tighten into itself until a small ring formed that then became an opening. The hole enlarged to about a foot in diameter. Nothing happened. The form simply undulated like a mound of aluminum gelatin that had been jostled.

Without warning, grapefruit-sized beige spheres began to spew out of the orifice, hovering at an altitude of a few feet. Within seconds, a dozen had formed a line between the strange blob and the prone troops, followed by more in rapid succession.

"What the hell are you waiting for?" Troyer yelled into his mike. "Sergeant!"

CHAPTER 46

The scenes on the holotape unfolded on the screen in front of him. Masterson watched the rescue operation with fascination as the first members of Troyer's crew broke through the metal doors. He saw the chaos as the strange devices attacked and the fighting ensued—with Trent, Houston, and Banning getting out—along with some confused frames of Houston shooting into what appeared to be a giant shimmering tent inside the huge cavern. Because the pictures were taken by a helmet camera, there was a fair amount of jerkiness, but everything remained in focus, including the final pictures of the exploding site.

Ekstrom's narration gave no reasonable explanation for what Masterson had just seen.

"Aliens," Ekstrom had said. "Troyer and the others will explain everything."

When the video finished, Masterson, scowling with anger,

got up and pushed the eject button. He backed up, standing alone in the middle of his office, holding the cassette.

"What am I going to do with this?" he said aloud, returning to his chair. *I'm supposed to report to Mr. Trent and tell him some oversized blob of alien crap is responsible for the disappearance of two of his ships, their payloads and crews, the destruction of Geneva Station and a couple hundred people's lives, and then give him that news that his grandson will be charged with sabotage and murder in connection with it all? No. I could just hand him the tape and let him see for himself. Sure. And then tell him why I didn't tell him.*

"Shit," he snarled. Masterson urged himself out of the comfort of his overstuffed, high-back executive chair and left his office.

Draper's next phone call was to the Santa Barbara police. He explained who he was and summarized the events of the night before, purposely omitting any theories he had concerning the contraption in the big hall.

"These people need food and clothing," Draper told the desk sergeant. "They've been out there for days and have no clothes at all." He also mentioned the call from his wife and that they should have some kind of report on that, probably from the San Diego police.

The sergeant acknowledge Debbie's missing person call and that the authorities in San Diego had cancelled the alert. "We normally wouldn't have done anything for another full day anyway, Doctor," he said. "Now, how many people are in this group you're talking about?"

"About fifty. I don't know exactly, and a number of them are women. One woman, name of Darla Sanders, is more or less in charge."

"Well, we'll take enough clothing out there. I'll tell the crew to take jumpsuits, stretch type, so anybody can wear them. Now tell me exactly where they are."

Doctor Draper explained how to find the former captives. When he finished, he was assured the rescuers would be on their way in less than an hour.

"Anything else, Doctor?"

"Yes. Help them contact their kin. I'm sure a lot of people are just as worried as my wife was. Oh—and you might ask Sanders to return my shirt."

"Return your shirt?"

"Yeah. I loaned it to her."

There was a short pause. Draper was certain Engel was smiling at a small fantasy. "Okay. We'll take care of everything. How about yourself—you need anything?"

"No, but thanks, Sergeant." He decided to let him think what he wanted. "I'm in my vehicle, and I'll be heading home. Thanks again."

"Just part of my job. You drive carefully now."

Draper rang off and considered his next move. He realized he would need an ally and thought about talking to Cameron Lloyd.

Some things still perplexed him. He wondered where that

diabolical machine he had seen underground in the Nevada desert had come from. The machine was obviously the instrument that had been injecting people's brains. That explained how people from all over the country—and the world—ended up becoming afflicted. They had simply been abducted while on vacation in Las Vegas, probably in much the same way he himself had been. Sometime later, after they had been implanted, they were released to carry the thing around with them.

Whoever was doing all this understood a bit of psychology, too: taking people's clothes leaves them vulnerable. But then they had to be given their clothing back, and somehow their memories had to be purged of the incident. He remembered the elderly couple, Ben and Robin Mattox, and the three hours Mrs. Mattox mentioned during which her husband had been unaccounted for during their trip.

What also puzzled him was the explosion of sudden, apparently unmotivated and extremely vicious attacks, and the attempts at cannibalism. Even more baffling was that all the incidents seemed to have occurred at the same moment. He had no answers. He reconsidered making the call, but instead, he headed the car south on Interstate 15 toward San Diego and Kensington Laboratories where he met Doctor Lloyd in the lobby.

"We have to get to the lab where that sample is," Draper said. "It may hold the answer to everything that's been going on around here."

"Well, I did as you asked when we talked last. I put the

specimen in liquid oxygen and locked it up next to the Research Office. Let's go."

As they rode up in the elevator, Draper wondered when Pollie Houston could have encountered old Charlie in the desert or whatever circumstances led to her being injected with that thing. He made a mental note to ask Mark about it when he returned.

They arrived at the twelfth floor. Stepping out of the elevator, they headed toward the Research Office, Lloyd's territory at Kensington. The door to large room had a warning sign:

For Access Contact Dr. Cameron Lloyd.

Inside, Draper saw that the office housed several cabinets and containers used for the various projects going on at any one time. Lloyd stepped past the first row and approached a large stainless steel drum in the middle of the second row. He stopped in front of the drum, worked a keypad in front of it, and the top popped open amidst a cloud of white haze. Lloyd pulled a thick leather glove onto his right hand and reached inside. He withdrew a small, round, metal container and put it on the marble stand next to the drum. He attached two small sensors to opposite sides of the can and flipped a switch. Two microlasers began to scan the object, a slow procedure designed to bring it to room temperature. During the process, Draper looked at Lloyd, who glanced at him once than gazed at the container. After a full minute, the sensor signal buzzed.

Lloyd grinned. "Dinner is served."

Draper picked up the container and brought it to the larger table in the middle of the room. Under the strong light, he carefully separated the two halves of the cylinder and inverted the bottom half.

A powdery brown dust poured out from the can. The dust was so fine it seemed to move in slow motion, like a fluid within a fluid. Stunned, both men watched as the wisps of microscopic particles wafted about like little brown ghosts in the miniscule movement of air.

They looked at each other, neither daring to breathe. With painstaking slowness, Lloyd lifted his open hand toward the other man. "Go easy, Doctor Draper," he said in a voice just above a whisper, "and turn off the air conditioner—there, by the door."

Draper glanced at the control switch and backed toward it. His gaze turned to the smoky substance dancing in a precarious cloud above the white surface in front of them, but he knew it was too late.

At the edge of the counter, the almost imperceptible breeze from the air exchanger captured the swirling remains of Doctor Draper's quest. Before their eyes, the brown vapors were caught up in the mixture of moving molecules. Helpless to do anything about it, they watched as the stringy remains faded in an excruciating, inexorable blend, then were rendered invisible, and finally became an indistinguishable part of the mass of air in the room. In the next few seconds, the brown vapors were sucked into the hospital's ventilation system, undeterred by the filters, to become but another minute consideration in the San Diego Air Quality Management Department statistics for the day.

Draper slammed the empty can on the ceramic surface, a grimace of deep anger on his face. "Damn!"

CHAPTER 47

The first meteor, a great boulder weighing three thousand tons, slowed slightly as it encountered the mixture of methane and nitrogen at the upper levels of the Titan atmosphere. The meteor began to rotate, its leading edge reddening from the heat of friction. Following the first by a few seconds was a group of a dozen more, ranging in size from forty feet across to almost the size of a football field. They were spread apart more or less evenly, as though they had been thrown by some gigantic hand. Following the initial meteor, each started to roll, its surface temperature increasing rapidly as it plunged into the denser layers of gases. More waves joined the angry procession speeding toward the single area of activity on the planet below.

Captain Hastings received the warning from his proximity alert and immediately realized they were being bombarded by the objects raining down directly at them from overhead. He punched his communications button. "Captain Troyer! Meteors!" At the same time, he applied full power to his ship, which instantly drove forward. The nearest of the cluster hurtled past where only seconds before the ship had been hovering. Eyes wide, Carole gripped the edge of the console in front of her. Mark sat in amazement, knowing he could do nothing. They watched as some of the projectiles at the outside of the first group changed their path, zeroing in on the ships and men on the ground.

"Jesus, that damned thing is controlling them!" Mark said.

"They won't have time," Hastings said.

The *Vikinghaul's* computer had already checked the projected track of the objects falling on them. Captain Troyer concluded there was no possibility of escape.

"Hawley!" he yelled into the radio. "Get the hell out of here!"

He jabbed his forefinger on the button in front of him. The *Vikinghaul's* engines came to life, their flames jetting out below, spraying huge clouds of dust and soil. Its great bulk straining, the spacecraft lifted from its berth and began to move over the planet's surface, closing the short distance between itself and the metallic globule. Troyer controlled the big cargo hauler's course perfectly, aiming its nose downward, exactly on target.

Hawley and his crew stopped to look up. Gigantic chunks of ore and ice streamed at them from the sky as the huge ship bore down on them from the left. They had no time to move.

The *Vikinghaul* was struck just behind the bridge at the same instant it slammed into the ground. The huge rock's rotation continued after impact, smashing the ship as if it were under some monstrous rolling pin. The *Vikinghaul's* sides split and gave way under the tremendous weight and pressure, crushing every floor, ceiling, and bulkhead. The *Vikinghaul* made direct hits on the guardians and the mercurial blob, but also on Sergeant Hawley and his troops on the ground below. The drive engines exploded with colossal force, spewing a gigantic expanding circle of blue-white flames, creating a twenty-foot deep crater. Both the *Baronhaul* and the *Princesshaul* were torn apart by the blast.

Captain Lisa Ingersoll had just begun liftoff. The *Stellarhaul*, struggling to move out of harm's way, was not quite fast enough. The edge of the conflagration caught the ship, and the concussion caused her to lurch at an angle, plowing into the Titan sand and rocks nose first. The *Stellarhaul* heeled onto her side and was teetering at the vertical when the next meteors crashed down. Struck simultaneously by three meteors, the ship disintegrated beneath them in a second massive explosion.

The *Mastiff*, its main thrusters at full, kept just ahead of the roiling debris and shock waves from the colossal eruptions on the surface. Reaching escape velocity, it sped like a bullet out of the Titan atmosphere, leaving the tortuous scene of destruction and carnage behind. For many minutes, the *Mastiff* continued to accelerate into the blackness of space.

No one on board spoke.

CHAPTER 48

Captain Hastings worked the controls in silence, altering their course to slip under the whirling Saturnian disc and onto a heading for Earth and home. When the trajectory was confirmed, he entered the datum and shut the main engines down. He then began to recount the tragic events of the past hours verbally into the ship's log.

Still clenching the slanted console in front of him, Mark stared ahead, unseeing. He had not moved since the ship began to evade the first meteor. His mind was still reeling from the enormity that had taken place only moments ago, and, like a movie playback, the sights and sounds continued inside his head.

He turned his gaze to his right and saw Carole, sitting rigidly, her head bowed. She, too, must have been mesmerized by the tragedy she watched unfold. After a moment, as though she sensed he was looking at her, she turned slowly toward him and opened her mouth as if to say something, but spoke not a word.

Having finished his log entries, Hastings stood. "We've got a long way to go. You two better make preparations and get into your pods."

They got to their feet. "I'm ready for that," Mark said.

The trio was headed toward the bridge exit when they were startled by an urgent beeping from the captain's console. Captain Hastings dashed back to his control position and punched in an inquiry. The screen in front of him sprang to life, zeroing in on the cause for the signal. While Mark and Carole scrambled back into their seats, Hastings added the visual to their terminals.

Above them less than fifty miles ahead, a huge circular opening had formed in Saturn's rotating rings. A large spherical object with a smooth, windowless, brown-metallic surface began descending toward them through the hole. Graphics filled the lower portion of the screen:

Speed:125 miles per hour
    Distance:48.6 miles
    Diameter:92 feet
    Composition:unknown
    Life signs:None. NO response to communication query.
    Recommendations:Alert Condition.

• • •

Hastings fired up the *Mastiff's* rocket motors and armed the ship's weapons system.

The mysterious bulk passed through the gap in the ring just as the *Mastiff* slipped under it, whereupon the bulk changed course and began to follow like a bloodhound that has come upon the trail of a rabbit. Within seconds the mysterious bulk matched and then exceeded the *Mastiff's* speed, diminishing the distance between them to less than two hundred miles.

"We have a tail," the captain said, "and I don't know what the hell it is. Banning, are you familiar with that interrogation system?"

Carole scanned the board in front of her. "Yes, sir."

"See if you can get any other readings on that object, especially if it has any weapons."

For each of the procedures Carole tried, the computer repeated its previous information with only the distance and speed of the unknown object changing as it bore down on them. She relayed the results to Hastings.

"That's got to be Immana's mother ship," Mark said. "Remember, we didn't get any lifeform readings back at the site, either—and it's catching up with us."

"I see that, Mr. Houston," Hastings said. "Hold on."

With a few quick entries on the control panel, he cut the *Mastiff's* main engine and spun the craft around to face their antagonist. The giant metallic globe did not alter its course but continued closing on the *Mastiff* with alarming speed.

Hastings waited until the sphere was less than ten miles away, and the screen was almost filled with its mass. All three watched as an orifice several feet wide opened in the center of the curved surface facing them. A dozen familiar round objects burst out, as if shot from a cannon. As soon as the last round object cleared, the opening began to close.

Captain Hastings did not hesitate. He aimed and fired the plasma cannon directly into the hole. As the globes scattered to avoid the shot, the pulsating yellow beam was swallowed by the darkness inside the sphere. At the same moment, the program Hastings had punched into his console powered up his ship The *Mastiff* lurched back toward the huge sphere and veered below its path, streaking beneath it only a few hundred yards away. The globe was in the process of turning to pursue the *Mastiff* when the explosion occurred.

CHAPTER 49

The tremendous white flash momentarily blanked out all the terminal screens. Outside the fireball itself, the *Mastiff* was barely able to outrun the cloud of debris that rocketed away from the disintegrating alien vessel. Two seconds later, the monitors came back online, and Hastings immediately punched in *visual to the rear*. The screen showed only a tiny, diminishing red point squarely in its center. The readings indicated thousands of bits and pieces of junk, but showed no further danger, and the distances were increasing.

"C'mon, baby, go!" Hastings growled, imploring his straining ship. His white-knuckled grip on the console relaxed as the safety margin became greater. After several seconds, he sat back and breathed a sigh of relief.

"Beautiful," Carole said. "That was the damnedest maneuver I've ever seen."

Mark relaxed his grip on the console in front of him and smiled. "When you were heading back towards that thing, I thought you'd lost your mind."

"Well," Hastings said, "I knew I couldn't outrun 'em, so I could only pray that coming back straight at 'em would give me the chance I needed. They just weren't quick enough, or the tactic wasn't in their manual."

"If you decide to risk all our lives again," Mark said, "would you please consult with us first?" He shook his head, but his grin betrayed his admiration. "I'll tell you one thing: when I put my feet back on that big blue marble once more, it's going to take a lot to get me off it."

Relieved, Hastings laughed. "I read you, loud and clear. You guys ready to go home?"

"Roger that," Carole said.

Course corrections returned them to their original headings. As soon as the *Mastiff* stabilized, Hastings added the appropriate supplement to his log.

Mark felt his own mood changing. He sat, eyes closed, frowning, his mind in turmoil thinking of the lives lost: Rico and the other *Sentinel* crew members; Troyer and his people; the terrible fate the people at Geneva Station endured.

And Eli.

Eli, your grandfather's going to kill you.

He snorted softly and lowered his face onto this folded arms, feeling tired and empty.

Carole noticed him. She paused, then left her seat and laid her hand lightly on his shoulder. "Mark? You okay?"

Slowly he turned to face her. Her gentle touch made him glad she was there. The emptiness began to leave him, replaced by the same comfort he always felt when he was with her. "Yeah," he said, getting up from his chair. "Thank you."

She smiled at him and took his hand.

They left the bridge together.

96194989R00142